'Are we going to tell Hugh about our relationship?'

An uneasy silence fell for a moment before Gina replied with characteristic frankness, 'I simply told him I was divorced. He accepted the fact without question.'

'I did that too. The matter hasn't been taken any further. Hugh makes up his mind about people without reservations—he either likes and instinctively trusts them, or he doesn't. His accepting you so promptly bears testimony.'

'It was a mutual response.'

Their eyes met and lingered. Tension built up in the wake of remembrance.

'Shall we leave it at that?' The question was a little breathless, and there was an unconscious note of appeal in it. Gina waited apprehensively for Adrian's answer, aware that his jawline hardened and he became slightly authoritative.

'That rather depends.' The statement seemed loaded.

'On what?' She looked anxious.

Adrian didn't hesitate as he said frankly, 'The type of relationship we can sustain, Gina.'

Sonia Deane is a widow with one son, lives in the Cotswolds, and has written over 120 books. The Medical Romances were fortuitous. She chose a doctor hero and from then on her readers wanted a medical background. Having personal friends who are doctors enables Sonia Deane's research to be verified. She has also been out with an ambulance team and donned a white coat in a hospital.

Previous Titles

DOCTOR ON CALL
DOCTOR ACCUSED

REPEAT PRESCRIPTION

BY

SONIA DEANE

MILLS & BOON LIMITED
ETON HOUSE   18–24 PARADISE ROAD
RICHMOND   SURREY   TW9 1SR

*First published in Great Britain 1991
by Mills & Boon Limited*

© Sonia Deane 1991

*Australian copyright 1991
Philippine copyright 1991
This edition 1991*

ISBN 0 263 77146 6

*Set in 10 on 12 pt Linotron Times
03-9102-50555
Typeset in Great Britain by Centracet, Cambridge
Made and printed in Great Britain*

CHAPTER ONE

DR GINA GORDON stared, shocked and disbelieving, as a tall familiar figure moved towards her and Mr Hugh Fawcett, surgeon, and head of the practice, said, 'Let me introduce my partner, Dr Marland. Now you're joining us, we shall be working closely together.'

Gina met the incredulous gaze of her ex-husband.

In that dramatic second, memories rushed back of their stormy, often ecstatic marriage that had ended after two years with an amicable parting because of the irretrievable breakdown of the relationship. Gina felt again the shattering pain and saw the shadow of Erin Foster who, while she had not figured in the case, stood seemingly in silent challenge as a medical secretary at the Royal Hospital in London, Adrian being senior registrar there. Gina had worked in a group practice in Kensington, where they had a flat in which she had continued to live until recently.

Adrian said, his voice deep, the intonation fascinating, 'Welcome, Dr Gordon. I hope you'll be very happy here.'

His handshake was firm and she was acutely conscious of his touch. Emotion robbed her of coherent thought and her mouth was dry as she managed to murmur, 'Thank you.'

For a second their eyes met in a look of startled amazement which became guarded as they realised Hugh Fawcett was watching them enquiringly. Gina added swiftly, 'I've always wanted to work here, in Chipping Campden. Gloucestershire is such a beautiful county.'

She wasn't aware of the importance she gave to her words. She and Adrian had dreamed—in their happy moments—of practising together there. Now she was conscious of his expressive dark grey eyes, that challenged in moments of argument, and of the way his dark brown hair curved into a single wave as it grew back from his forehead above well-marked brows. He had a smooth tan and his mouth was firm with a suggestion of humour at the corners. It registered subconsciously that he had not put on any weight, and that his broad shoulders emphasised his lithe body. He was an undeniably attractive man of thirty whom women found difficult to resist. But the hurt of the past stabbed, and she wanted to run away from the delicate situation implicit in their future contact. The acceptance of their divorce suddenly slid away and turmoil crept stealthily back. She felt like someone trying to run up a moving staircase that was on its way down.

Adrian continued, speaking with confidence, his manner easy, 'We badly need a woman to rescue us. You'll be a godsend, Dr Gordon.'

Tension mounted and then passed. Hugh Fawcett beamed. For an uncomfortable second he had feared lest these two might be incompatible.

'I hope your assessment may prove correct,' Gina said hopefully.

'And Dr Gordon is free to start at once.' Hugh Fawcett's voice was eager, his attitude bright—a brightness that typified his character, since he loved life, was forty-eight, with an endearing personality which inspired confidence and made him the surgeon everyone believed could work miracles. If Mr Fawcett was going to 'do the operation', then all would be well.

Adrian was not conscious of the fact that he didn't take his gaze from Gina's face as Hugh Fawcett talked about Gina meeting his wife, Anne, and his only child—an eighteen-year-old daughter, named Jill. It struck Adrian that Gina was more beautiful than he remembered her, and that she looked young for her twenty-six years. Her golden hair waved softly at chin length, like silk; her expressive deep blue-grey eyes illumined her face and betrayed every shade of expression. The gentle curves of her firm young breasts and unusually slim waist were emphasised by a wide belt that divided a tucked white blouse and navy skirt, just right for the exceptionally warm May day. He felt a sudden annoyance because of their parting and an irritation that she had now suddenly crashed into his life to destroy its tranquillity. Yet, he argued, there was no reason why they should fraternise outside the practice. The thought comforted him a little. They would certainly have to meet to discuss the format so far as Hugh Fawcett was concerned, and that would be that.

The initial shock was over and conversation flowed normally during the next few minutes when Gina explained that she had moved into a small flat only that week, near the Market Hall for which Chipping Campden was famous, standing in the centre of the imposing main street which had often been described as 'the most beautiful village street in England', its impressive arches giving views over the whole area, and kept in the care of the National Trust.

'I was determined to come to live here,' Gina explained. 'I argued that being five miles from Broadway, twenty-two from Cheltenham and only twelve from Stratford-upon-Avon, I was bound to get a job within those distances.'

'A very resolute young lady,' Adrian said with a wry expression.

Hugh Fawcett laughed. 'Fortunately for us!'

Gina looked directly into Adrian's eyes. 'I hate indecision and I'd had enough of London.' She added with enthusiasm, 'Mellow Cotswold stone appeals to me.'

'And to me,' Adrian said almost deliberately.

An unexpected caller wanting a word with Hugh Fawcett, and his going out into the hall to speak to her gave Adrian an opportunity to say swiftly to Gina, 'We must talk. Give me your address. Would seven this evening suit you?'

She didn't argue, but gave him a change-of-address card which she had in her handbag. 'Seven,' she said in a businesslike tone, then, as she heard Hugh Fawcett returning, went on, 'I like the way this house, Mill Lodge, has been converted so that the practice quarters are modern, but the rest is half timbered.'

'Best of both worlds,' Hugh Fawcett exclaimed with satisfaction. 'Not a bad policy!' His chuckle was infectious. 'And Adrian has a house not more than a few minutes away. We're practically in the High Street on the Ebrington Road. Nothing like proximity. . .' He added encouragingly, 'I'd like you to come along tomorrow and meet the staff, and get a more comprehensive idea of the layout of the practice.' In truth Hugh Fawcett had been so impressed with Gina, after a dismal trail of applicants, that he had been precipitate in engaging her with a view of future partnership. Adrian had left the matter entirely in his hands and had been on a spring holiday during the past fortnight. He too had come into the practice at short notice after the sudden death of Hugh Fawcett's previous partner, as a result of a coronary.

Gina was relieved to leave the house. She was trembling and uncertain as she got into her car and drove the short distance to her flat, aware that if anyone had told her she would meet her divorced husband that morning she would have regarded it as ridiculous. Now the possibility of seeing him that evening filled her with apprehension. She had put the divorce behind her as though it were part of another life, and had settled into a pleasant, if unemotional, routine which had been balm after the wounds and trauma of the separation. The word 'amicable' could justify its use, but not touch the heart of the matter.

Her flat had a new significance as she walked into it a few minutes later. She had retained the furniture from Kensington, and it suddenly seemed to acquire a personality of its own, representing something she had forgotten. She gazed around critically. Dove-grey and cherry predominated, for it had been converted, and furnishings to tone with half-timbered walls would not have been in order. It was, in fact, a replica of their London home, although she had never realised it until that moment. She stood in the centre of the sitting-room a little helplessly, frankly scared at the situation she now faced. It was enough to be starting in a new practice with the possibility of a partnership, let alone facing up to working with Adrian.

Did she want a coffee? It was too near lunchtime and she didn't feel like eating; and she didn't quite know what she was going to do with the hours until seven o'clock. The fact annoyed her. So—she had to face up to a difficult situation. Was that any reason to panic? She told herself angrily that she had never done so before, and decided that her prized pieces of silver looked dull and could do with a clean. Work was the panacea for all ills. At that moment she found herself shrinking from her own weakness, the very idea of doing anything special because Adrian was coming seeming ludicrous. The flowers were freshly arranged. A small silver cabinet had pride of place on one wall and deep armchairs offered relaxation. A circular table covered with dove-grey silk which touched the ground, over which a pale cherry cloth was draped, completed the picture. Photographs stood on the top.

Adrian arrived promptly at seven. Gina admitted him with an air of unreality as though her mind had drifted away from her body and nothing was real. He had changed into a light grey suit that suggested a more casual air, and his blue shirt suited his tan. The hallway was narrow, and as she closed the front door they stood close for a second before she led the way into the sitting-room in silence. She was acutely nervous, but found it impossible to judge his reactions.

Having glanced around him, he said almost involuntarily, 'You've made this very attractive, but you always had a flair for achieving that result.'

The utterance was a simple statement of fact, and she accepted it with a murmured, 'Thank you.' As she sat down she indicated the chair opposite and said, 'Can I offer you a drink?'

'A small whisky would be very welcome.'

She poured it out from the decanter on the silver drinks tray which, as he watched, Adrian recalled, because both decanter and tray had been given to them by her parents. She tried to keep her hands steady as he got to his feet and hovered at her side. Finally he took his whisky and her sherry, and placed them on their respective side-tables by the chairs. Seated again, they nodded as they took their first sip, the tension easing slightly. Their gaze met directly and his eyes darkened in their appraisal, his personality electrifying.

'So finally we've both arrived at Chipping Campden by different routes,' he said, his voice having a haunting intonation.

But the thought that dominated Gina was the possibility that he was still seeing Erin, and the question automatically followed: Why hadn't they married? Emotion made her tremble, and it was an effort to keep her hand steady enough to raise her glass. Antagonism crept in.

'Quite dramatic.' Her words were clipped.

Adrian noticed her attractive white dress, elegant in its simplicity. She had not, he thought, lost her flair for clothes and her skin was still as smooth as a camellia. In fact he could not deny that she was beautiful and unusual. Somehow the fact annoyed him. Their divorce seemed ridiculous. Why in hell couldn't they have made a go of their marriage? he asked himself irritably.

'Mr Fawcett was very anxious to get things settled,' she said, her eyes meeting his in faint challenge.

'He'd seen so many unsuitable people.' Adrian sat back a little deeper in his chair and crossed one leg over the other. She was aware of the gesture with a physical reaction, and words raced through her head. It was *Adrian* sitting there. The man she had loved, married and slept with, knowing his body as intimately as her own, sharing the ecstasy of sexual fulfilment as well as the fierce anger of dissension. He was also, she reflected, the first and only man with whom she had made love.

At that moment Adrian said, coming straight to the point, 'Are we going to tell Hugh about our relationship?' He dropped his gaze and then looked at her disarmingly.

An uneasy silence fell for a moment before she replied with characteristic frankness, 'I simply told him I was divorced. He accepted the fact without question.'

'I did that too. The matter hasn't been taken any further. Hugh makes up his mind about people without reservations—he either likes and instinctively trusts them, or he doesn't. His accepting you so promptly bears testimony.'

'It was a mutual response.'

Their eyes met and lingered. Tension built up in the wake of remembrance.

'Shall we leave it at that?' The question was a little breathless, and there was an unconscious note of appeal in it. Gina waited apprehensively for his answer, aware that his jawline hardened and he became slightly authoritative.

'That rather depends.' The statement seemed loaded.

'On what?' She looked anxious.

He didn't hesitate as he said frankly, 'The type of relationship we can sustain, Gina.'

The use of her name changed the atmosphere and

sent a tremor over her, bringing an intimacy for which she was not prepared.

'Meaning?' Her voice was low. She waited in suspense.

The silence of the room deepened; the evening sun sent shafts of golden light on to the furniture, glinting on silver and the cut-glass flower vase. And although it was an unusually warm evening for May she shivered, her nerves taut.

'If we can ignore the past and have a professional——' he hesitated, searching for the right words, before adding, 'Professional friendliness.'

She stiffened and said somewhat tersely, 'Without any question of actual *friendship*.'

He shook his head. 'I didn't mean it quite like that.'

'It isn't easy,' she said involuntarily. 'We're bound to be drawn into social contacts. As I see it, if we understand each other there shouldn't be any problems.'

His gaze was an assessment as he said meaningly, 'Ah! Understanding is a big word.'

She reminded him with an unconscious note of nostalgia, 'It enabled us to be divorced without bitterness.'

They lapsed into silence which he broke by reminding her, 'But we haven't seen each other since then.' His gaze was unnerving.

She said with a touch of impulsiveness, 'Would it be better if I backed out? I——'

He cut in, 'Let's face this challenge! We gave in the first time, and, while this is quite different, I'd like to think we could make it work.'

Emotion from which they both retreated neverthe-less drove them to silence, which he broke by saying, 'This all seems very unreal.'

Just then the thought of Erin flashed through Gina's mind. Again she wondered about their relationship and whether Erin was still in Adrian's life, in no matter what capacity; but she refrained from questioning, not wanting to highlight the past. Adrian was not the type of man to volunteer any information that affected him personally. But the fact that he had not remarried intrigued her. For although she had no justification for associating him intimately with Erin, she could not deny that the tiny flame of jealousy had nevertheless burned, and even her name, now, brought a strange reaction, which she recognised as absurd.

'The cliché that truth is stranger than fiction is always valid.'

He nodded his agreement and then said, almost urgently, 'What have you been doing? I'd like to know.'

She told him how she had stayed on in the Kensington practice and flat, the lease and contents of which he had readily made over to her. 'Then,' she went on, 'I decided that I'd make a complete break and leave London. And the goal hadn't changed,' she said firmly. 'Chipping Campden was to be my destiny. I've been staying with a friend, Maggie Latham, in Stratford-upon-Avon until I found this flat. I needed a rest and could have remained with her as long as I liked. I didn't worry about joining a practice, deciding that I'd wait until I was settled in my own home. This flat came out of the blue because the owner was

suddenly posted abroad, and the price wasn't exorbi-
tant, as he wanted a quick sale. I'd only had time to
get settled in when I saw Mr Fawcett's advert
and. . .well, you know the rest. My parents are of
course in Dunster, and my Father is still the favourite
dentist in Minehead.' She added, 'And Mother is
delighted that I'm out of London.' She added deliberately, 'And what about you?'

'A rather similar pattern,' Adrian said with a half-
smile. 'I decided to take the plunge and get away from
London and hospital life. You have the advantage of
previously being in general practice; it was a step in the
dark for me. But Hugh's partner had died and as I was
looking around here, wanting to settle. . . We've been
faithful to our dreams,' he added, his voice low, his
gaze penetrating, 'of practising in Chipping Campden.'

'A curious irony.' She lifted her chin and threaded
her fingers through her soft, shining hair—a little
mannerism which he noticed and which brought back
memories. 'I wouldn't like to feel we were *deceiving*
Mr Fawcett without justifiable reasons.' The words
came swiftly, and again they looked at each other,
seeking guidance.

'He might feel awkward if he knew—that's the
point,' said Adrian. 'And so might we. I want to get
the practice working smoothly. He's been through a
lot, Gina. The loss of Guy, his partner, was a great
blow after ten years. Now we've settled into a very
good relationship, even in a year. With you, provided
we can work amicably together, things could be ideal.'
He added genuinely, 'He's a splendid person. I'd hate
to spoil his enthusiasm, or give him any worry.'

Gina appreciated the sentiments and said gently, 'Then we must live up to his expectations.'

'That means,' he said, looking at her intently, 'forgetting the past and working on a friendly basis.' There was meaning in the words.

Emotion touched them and she said significantly, 'You have no need to fear that I shall intrude in your life, Adrian.' The use of his name was deliberate. 'I shall be at Mill Lodge to work, and keep my part of the bargain. I certainly shan't expect any favours.' Her voice was firm, her manner almost brusque.

He remembered that flash in her dark eyes, the faint colour that heightened her normal attractive flush, and he said swiftly, 'Suppose we don't make an issue of it? That will defeat us. Our objectives are, I'm sure, the same. It should be an interesting experiment.'

Her pulse quickened slightly and she stared at him, his cool manner reminding her of other days when, after an argument, he would withdraw into a world of his own, without sullenness, which would infuriate her and always seem to put her in the wrong.

'I agree,' she said, meeting his gaze with a disarming directness, their awareness intensified as memories of the past flooded back.

He finished his drink and said swiftly, 'I've a terminal pneumonia to see. A ninety-year-old who's lived his life to the full——'

'And whom one hates to see go, even though it's the best way. . .'

The atmosphere changed and a wave of sympathetic understanding passed between them. They were on common ground, and the bond held.

'How true. . . Have you enjoyed your rest from work?'

Gina nodded and got to her feet. 'But I shall love getting back to it, starting a new life.'

He stood beside her. 'We really want your help, Gina. The practice is far too much for the two of us and we need a woman as well. You will, I assure you, be much appreciated.'

They met each other's gaze, and Gina was aware of his nearness as they moved towards the front door. A strange, almost bleak feeling surged over her as she opened it.

'I'll probably see you tomorrow when you come to take stock and meet the staff,' said Adrian.

'A formidable prospect.'

He laughed—a deep laugh that was infectious. 'Yes. . .liked by the patients and dreading a woman doctor in the practice!' He added, 'You'll soon win them over. Goodbye, Gina. I think we shall adapt quite well.'

Her smile was an answer.

It was not until he had gone that she realised how little she had learned about his actual life.

Gina absorbed the beauty of Chipping Campden as she set off for Mill Lodge the following morning, its gently curving High Street containing ancient buildings, some dating back to the thirteenth century, their mellow Cotswold stone glowing in the bright May sunshine, the grass verges at some points rising steeply to near-cobbled pavements, which emphasised the atmosphere of antiquity. And through her appreciation ran disjointed thoughts. Would she see Adrian? Would she be able to maintain a purely friendly attitude, never touching upon the intimacy that had been part of their life? It struck her suddenly that she still wore her wedding-ring and that it had not occurred to her to remove it. Had he noticed the fact? It was distinctive and chased; not too wide. She had put aside her engagement ring which, in any case, she would not wear during professional hours.

To her surprise Adrian opened the door to her.

'I just happened to see you arrive,' he explained. 'My room is at the front.'

Mill Lodge was a double-fronted Cotswold stone house built at a rather crazy angle which Hugh Fawcett had renovated internally to suit practice needs and give all modern comforts, without detracting from its original charm.

Gina murmured a greeting and he added, 'Surgery's over and I haven't started on my rounds yet. Hugh is at the Cheltenham General Hospital—an emergency appendix—so I've been detailed to look after you.'

'Oh!' Gina's lips were dry and she felt far more tense than on the previous evening. She tried desperately to relax and regard Adrian as someone with whom she would be working, and who would be her superior.

He led her to his room on the left of the square hall from which the practice quarters radiated. An impressive desk was given prominence, together with a bookcase filled with medical books and on top of which stood a vase of yellow and mauve tulips. Which one of the staff, Gina asked herself, had a crush on him?

He didn't indulge in any small talk as he said, 'Now let me introduce you to the rest of us.' He flicked down the intercom and said a few words. A few seconds later he introduced Irene Greyson, secretary, near retiring age, married, well upholstered and with a friendly manner to match her rosy cheeks. She had worked for Hugh Fawcett for twenty years. Next came Janet Westbury, a widow and Irene Greyson's assistant, tall, thin and pale, who had been in the practice for ten years and was now thirty-five. Lastly Nurse Avril Lane, twenty-eight, unmarried, smart in her uniform of blue and white—volatile, popular and a great asset.

'I'm sure,' Gina said, 'we shall all work harmoniously together.' And even as she appraised the three women, she decided that Janet Westbury had been responsible for the flowers.

Adrian gave a light laugh. 'You,' he said, his words embracing them all, 'will be four women to two men!'

Gina wondered what would happen if she were suddenly to say, 'And Dr Marland is my ex-husband!'

They talked for a few minutes, and then Adrian and Gina found themselves alone as the door closed behind them.

'They're a good team,' Adrian said warmly. 'We dread the thought of Irene Greyson retiring. Fortunately she doesn't refer to it. Her husband is retired, but as he's a golf fiend and remarkably young for his age her working suits them both. . . Oh, by the way, after I've shown you around, Anne, Hugh's wife, and his daughter Jill want you to join them for coffee.' He went on confidently, 'You'll like them. Jill is eighteen and just left college. You'll be able to help her. She doesn't want university life and is a bit of a problem.'

Gina noticed that Adrian talked with the familiarity of one whose assessment of her was precise, and made the past very real.

'Late teenagers are beset with problems these days,' she hastened to say.

He nodded and sighed. 'And we get the repercussions in our surgeries, as you must well know. . . Now what would you specially like to see?'

'My room,' she said immediately. 'I had only a brief glance at it.'

He took her out into the hall and opened a door to the right, standing aside for her to enter.

'You won't like it,' he said emphatically.

She flashed him a swift glance to suggest that he still seemed familiar with her tastes. Their arms touched as they moved towards the desk, and she was aware of him, his power overwhelming.

'I must say you're very right,' she admitted, taking in the scene around them, which was bleak and drab, with only the barest necessities of furniture.

He explained, 'We thought it would be a good idea to let the new assistant-cum-partner express her own personality here. We don't want a drawing-room, but a few feminine touches wouldn't come amiss.' He paused and added, 'You'll transform this without destroying its purpose.'

'You flatter me,' she said half admonishingly.

'Divorce didn't rob me of my memory,' he suggested, and looked at her intently, 'or my powers of observation.' His gaze went to her left hand. 'I notice you still wear your wedding-ring.' His voice was low and significant. Silence, deep and full of emotion, fell. Drama crept into the atmosphere, bringing past and present together in incredible juxtaposition.

She fingered the gold band. 'I shall only take it off

when I marry again,' she said with a rush of confidence. 'We didn't part as enemies.'

His gaze was intense. 'When you marry again,' he echoed abruptly. 'Are you thinking of doing so?'

She stared him out. There was a touch of defiance in her voice as she asked, 'Are you?' As she spoke, she was conscious of their surroundings and of the empty feel of the room, redeemed only by a view of the garden, bright with tulips, lilacs and laburnum. Apple trees, laden with snowy pink blossom, completed the picture of the beauty and richness of spring.

Adrian exclaimed shortly, 'You were always good at answering one question by asking another.'

'Then shall I say that I'm not averse to the possibility; it depends on whom one meets. Life can change in a minute, and coincidence, as we're proving, plays a large part.' She watched him carefully, but his manner was inscrutable and it provoked her, so that she said directly, 'At least I've answered *your* question.'

He looked away from her. 'I have no plans,' he said briefly, and the subject was closed.

They dealt with the necessities for the room.

'An upholstered patients' chair,' Gina insisted. 'Patients feel wretched enough when they consult me, without having to sit as though they're in a schoolroom. They're also mostly in pain of some description. . . Could I have a few bookshelves too? Books are furniture, as your room testifies.'

Adrian made an expansive gesture as he said, 'You have a free hand. I see your point.'

'It can be made welcoming.' She smiled with satisfaction. 'The little examining-room and cloakroom are splendid—far better than I've been accustomed to.'

She looked at the leaded windows and felt the pull of their antiquity. 'A blend of old and new——'

'When you've made it over,' he suggested, almost teasingly. It was a phrase he had so often used in the past, and their eyes met, their gaze lingering as memory stabbed.

The common-room, offices and surgery waiting-room were, Gina thought, above standard and comfortably practical, with white walls to dispel any gloom. She saw the staff again and then Adrian said, 'Now come and meet the others.' He took her through a corridor leading from the hall, into Hugh Fawcett's part of the house, calling out, 'Anne, we're here!'

Anne, forty-two, slim, wearing a pale grey cashmere jumper and pleated skirt of a darker shade, came forward with a wide, welcoming smile. She was the power behind the throne where Hugh Fawcett was concerned, and while she did not dominate him she subtly influenced him, always for his own good. She had well-groomed hair that framed a friendly face. Her eyes sparkled, her expression encouraging.

'Welcome, Dr Gordon; or since you're joining us, may I call you Gina? I'm Anne.'

Gina felt immediately at home as they went into a beautifully furnished sitting-room in shades of rose and old gold. Deep armchairs stood invitingly at the correct angles and a few antiques lent dignity to homeliness.

At that moment Jill, the daughter, joined them, saying with flamboyant cheerfulness, 'It'll be splendid to have you to help Daddy and Adrian. With luck we may see a little more of them, and of course we hope to see you too, Dr Gordon. I'm surrounded with doctors, but I haven't really one of my own.' She laughed. 'I'm on your list from this moment!'

Gina looked into faintly mysterious green-grey eyes, set in an elfin-type face framed with chestnut hair, waving naturally back from her forehead, and felt a strange sensation of apprehension. There was a contra-dictory air of sensuality about Jill, and Gina felt that her words, 'I'm on your list from this moment'. were prophetic.

Adrian was not aware that he stood close beside Gina, his manner unconsciously proprietorial.

Just as they were about to sit down, Jill cried, 'Hello, Malcolm!' as Malcolm Villiers came unceremoniously into the room. He was a general practitioner specialis-ing in obstetrics, who lived in Chipping Campden, and was a great friend of the Fawcetts. A good friend of Adrian too.

Adrian watched in the silence that followed his introduction to Gina, realising that sudden emotion had built up, and Malcolm's intense concentration was suggestive of a man who had fallen in love at first sight.

Gina extended her hand, and their gaze held as she greeted him.

CHAPTER TWO

GINA could not escape from the steady, almost bewildered look that Malcolm Villiers gave her; it was disturbing and faintly sensual. His blue eyes met hers in a gaze so revealing that emotion touched her. He was an attractive man of medium height and slight build, whose face glowed with health. His features were regular, his manner suggestive of good humour and frankness. His hair was light brown and well cut.

'I'm Malcolm,' he said, defying her to escape from his steady scrutiny, which she found unnerving. Subconsciously she was aware of Adrian's fleeting startled glance.

'And I'm Gina,' she replied.

Malcolm held her hand longer than was necessary and added as he let it go, 'We shall be seeing a great deal of each other.' He spoke prophetically and with confidence.

Anne, conscious of the tension, explained, 'This is Malcolm's second home.' It seemed to suffice as a comment on his remark. 'And I hope——' she smiled as she spoke '—you'll feel that it's yours too.'

Jill thrust herself forward and moved to Malcolm's side with a little proprietorial gesture. Her eyes were bright, but with a touch of suspicion in them. Malcolm continued to look at Gina as though mesmerised.

'I'm sure,' Gina said warmly to Anne, 'that it won't

be difficult to trespass on your kindness. I don't know anyone here.'

'Apart from present company,' said Adrian before a sudden silence fell.

Hugh Fawcett's voice calling out, 'Any coffee?' restored normality as he came blithely into the room. 'No complications with that one,' he added, addressing Adrian and speaking of the operation. Then looking from Malcolm to Gina he exclaimed, 'So you two have met?'

'Yes,' Malcolm said with quiet innuendo.

Gina began, 'Mr Fawcett——'

He interrupted her. 'No formality out of practice hours,' he insisted as he took the cup of coffee Anne handed to him from a nearby tray. 'I'm Hugh. How did you like your room, by the way?' He shot Adrian an amused look.

Adrian answered for Gina. 'She didn't, but——'

'But,' Gina rushed in, 'I like the room, and with a few changes——'

'Ah!' chuckled Hugh, flashing Anne a knowing look. 'Changes are always costly. . .but you shall have your way.' He glanced at Adrian for confirmation.

Adrian gave Gina a meaning smile. 'A woman usually does.'

'Sexist!' cried Jill explosively. She studied Adrian somewhat critically. 'I think you're a bit of a chauvinist.' Her gaze turned to Gina. 'Watch out: *you* don't know him. *We* do!' She added with a touch of humour, 'An unknown quantity!'

Gina gave a little laugh. 'Thank you for the warning.'

'Oh,' the sound was lofty, 'I may be young, but I know a *little* about men!'

'The confidence of inexperience,' Adrian said indulgently.

Jill gave a toss of her head as she retorted, 'Your remark proving my point.'

The gathering broke up a short while later. Malcolm manoeuvred so that he walked beside Gina to the communicating door which led to the practice quarters.

'Will you have dinner with me next week?' He spoke as a man not intending to be rebuffed.

She met his gaze in surprise, aware that Adrian was immediately behind them and could overhear the question.

'Thank you,' she said with sudden confidence and a touch of defiance, 'I'd like to.'

They had now reached the hall by the surgery. Malcolm added, 'If you'll give me your telephone number, I'll ring you to finalise things.'

She told him, suggesting that he would not remember it.

'On the contrary, it's one I shall never forget,' he assured her, his gaze direct as he left them.

Hugh hurried off to his consulting-room, and Adrian and Gina stood alone.

'You've certainly made a conquest.' Adrian's voice was low and suggestive.

'I like him.' She spoke frankly. 'Nothing complicated.'

They looked at each other speculatively.

'Meaning that I was?' The words came a trifle sharply.

'Meaning that I wasn't talking about us. Yesterday's dead.'

He persisted, 'Then will you have dinner with me on

a day of your choosing? That will take us into tomorrow.' He was amazed by his own impulsiveness.

Her smile was provocative. 'Ask me again when I've worked for you a little while,' she replied guardedly.

Nurse Lane hurried towards them. 'We've got a bad arm burn, Dr Marland. I need your advice.' She glanced half apologetically at Gina for interrupting the conversation.

Adrian immediately departed.

Gina's room took only a matter of days to renovate, and she started work the following Monday. Hugh said easily, 'I'm going to let you deal with Adrian. He can show you the ropes and select your list. If you've any major problems then come along to me and we'll sort them out.' He looked at her indulgently. 'And don't forget that you're always welcome to the house—without any formality.'

'You've already made me welcome,' she said appreciatively.

'Anne has taken to you,' he admitted with a gleam of satisfaction in his eyes. It was obvious that he had a great respect for his wife's judgement.

Adrian stood by his desk as Gina entered his room for briefing a little later. He indicated the patients' chair and they both sat down, he leaning slightly forward, his hands clasped loosely on his blotting-pad.

'You'll find this a cosmopolitan practice,' he began, adding swiftly, 'oh, I know that could describe many practices, but we get a great number of visitors here, so that the population varies. We treat quite a few patients from abroad who are taken ill while on holiday and it's a good thing to brush up on the less familiar complaints.' His voice was smooth, his gaze impersonal.

Gina said composedly, 'We came up against that problem where I was before, but I appreciate what you mean. It's not surprising that there's a reaction to our climate.'

He stiffened slightly and sat back in his chair. 'That's rather an over-simplification.'

Faint annoyance quickened her pulse. She might be doing him an injustice, but she felt he was pulling rank, and in the circumstances she resented the fact. This man had been her *husband*. She reminded herself, anger just beneath the surface, that this was no longer true and she would do well to remember the fact.

'Then,' she said coolly, 'I didn't make myself clear. I'll bear what you say in mind.'

'I just wanted to put you in the picture.'

There was a moment's heavy silence; they were conscious of each other as tension mounted. Adrian noticed the way her hair shone in the sunlight that struck from the window behind her, and in turn she thought how immaculate he looked with a white shirt emphasising his tan.

'I'd like you,' he told her, 'to take over several midder cases and relieve me of some of the gynae problems.'

Gina stared him out. She didn't want to be merely an assistant, although at this stage it was technically her title—with a view to partnership.

'Don't worry,' he said immediately, reading her thoughts, 'you won't be in danger of becoming a dogsbody.'

She wanted to say, 'You know me too well,' but

there was a dangerous element in the observation, so instead she smiled—a smile that transformed her face, making it even more attractive—as she said, 'I'm quite ready to help in order to succeed.'

He looked suddenly solemn. 'I didn't quite realise how habit dies hard. I haven't forgotten your reactions.' Emotion flared as he changed the subject. 'When are you having dinner with Malcolm?'

It was the last thing she expected him to ask.

'On Wednesday.'

'Are you in the habit of dining with strangers?' The question came startlingly.

She said a little sharply, 'I don't consider him a stranger in the sense that you imply. He's a friend of the Fawcetts, and your colleague. I've no doubt that you also met him through them.'

'*Touché!*'

She made a gesture to suggest that she must leave. 'I'm seeing Jill at nine,' she explained. 'My first patient. She made the appointment through Mrs Greyson. . . Mrs Greyson certainly seems the proverbial treasure.'

'The really indispensable secretary,' he agreed, pausing before adding, 'And, Gina——' The utterance of her name held a note of urgency.

'Yes?' she exclaimed in a breath.

'Don't forget that I'm here if you have any problems.' He hesitated for a moment. 'I'd like to feel that you'd consult me if necessary and not be put off by the past.'

Their eyes met as she got to her feet, and he to his.

'Thank you. I shall never take the past into account, I assure you, and will certainly be glad of your guidance should the necessity arise.' She was aware that her words sounded stilted, but she did not want to touch the edge of emotion.

Adrian watched her go, conscious of the litheness of her movements, her shapely legs and slim ankles. She managed to make even a white coat look smart. At the door, which he opened for her, she looked up at him with an awareness neither of them could ignore.

The intercom went and they parted hurriedly. She went to her room and sat at her desk, staring ahead as she tried to forget yesterday, annoyed that it should even be necessary.

Jill came in almost boldly a few minutes later. She was wearing a rather large lightweight cream jumper and a full scarlet skirt. She had poise and confidence, and appeared to be very sure of herself.

Gina emptied her mind of everything but the fact that she was now 'the doctor', but the last conscious thought was of Erin Foster's name, before she said, 'I must say you look very fit to be consulting me.'

Jill smiled broadly. 'I am fit. I told my mother it was just one of those period things. Covers a multitude of sins.' Her laughter was light and a little tantalising. '*Literally!*' She went on, 'I'm so glad you've joined us. I can now be your patient on a proper footing. I've never needed medical help, and you know how vague doctors are when it comes to their own family. It's almost an affront for any member to be ill.'

Gina was not deceived. Jill was playing for time.

'Suppose you tell me how I can help you.' Gina met her gaze very steadily and with a certain challenge.

There was a second of heavy silence before the words came firmly. 'I want to go on the pill.' Defiance strengthened her voice as she spoke.

The statement was so familiar that Gina told herself it was ridiculous to be surprised, particularly as there was a challenging modernity about Jill that was disconcerting.

'At this moment,' Jill hastened, 'I have no emotional ties, but I want to be prepared. I may as well add that I have no intention of sleeping around. It's far too dangerous these days, with AIDS to consider.'

Gina nodded her agreement.

'My parents have brought me up very sensibly,' Jill went on with a faintly patronising air, 'but naturally I don't want them to know my views, or my life.' Defiance crept into her expression. 'I'm a bit of a problem to them over university, but I feel much older than my years. . . What do you think of Malcolm?' It was a direct and unexpected question.

Gina knew that she had to show her authority and said firmly, 'I really don't see that my reactions are of any consequence.'

'They are to me. You're new on the scene, and he was like a man who'd fallen in love at first sight. I'm not blind, but I don't mind admitting that I have a crush on Malcolm and would go to bed with him tomorrow if he didn't see me as the *child* of his friend. . . Do I shock you?'

'Why are you trying so hard to do so? You, more than anyone, should know that doctors are shockproof. *Sometimes* surprised——'

'Do I surprise you?'

'Not after having listened to you for a few minutes,' Gina said coolly.

'I knew,' Jill said complacently, 'that I should like you.' She added with a smile, 'I can't think why anyone goes in for medicine. The very thought of it appals me. . . You *will* put me on the pill?' she added, and for the first time an earnest note crept into her voice.

'I'd rather not,' Gina said honestly. 'Unless you have a stable relationship, the later you start taking it the better, and at your age——' She knew the words were fatal the moment she had uttered them.

'*My* age! I'm *eighteen*. An adult in charge of my own life.'

'I'm aware of all that,' Gina said with quiet resoluteness, 'and I'm speaking purely as a doctor. That's one side of the story: the other is that if you intend to sleep with anyone before you're married, then it's right for me to protect you.'

Jill laughed softly. 'I don't see myself as the little virgin going up the aisle in white! On the other hand, I have standards and I'm fastidious.'

Gina did not make the mistake of praising her for the fact. Her reference to Malcolm was disconcerting, and Gina wondered if he had any notion of her feelings.

'I'd like to check your blood-pressure, heart and pulse,' Gina went on coolly. 'By the way, how are your periods?'

'Regular—no problem. I just fibbed to Mummy.' She added, 'Daddy seemed to assume the usual. I could have gone to Adrian——'

Gina said involuntarily, 'Why didn't you?' It seemed important to know.

'He's too involved with my father. I didn't want to place him in an invidious position. Also, he's an unknown factor. Not secretive exactly, but inscrutable. I can't judge his reactions to me. You, being new, are ideal.'

Gina was intrigued and allowed herself to be drawn into a discussion as she exclaimed, 'Why do you think of Dr Marland as the "unknown factor"?'

'Probably because he's a little mysterious. It's attractive. In fact he's a very attractive man, but never *quite* in the circle. Those dark X-ray eyes of his are disconcerting. Oh, he's always charming to me—and the patients rave about him. He's loaded with sex appeal because in so many ways he's remote. You'll discover that when you know him better.' She gave a little laugh which was part of a nervous reaction. 'He thinks I should go to university and get a degree—a kind of insurance for the future.'

Gina had taken the sphygmomanometer and prepared to check Jill's blood-pressure. She said briskly, 'Now let's see about you.'

Jill rolled up her sleeve and held out her arm. She knew the conversation had finished.

When the tests had been made and Jill was declared fit, Gina said with a quiet impressiveness, 'Don't rush into any relationship because you think it's safe. I'm doing this as the lesser of two evils. I'd be happier if you waited until you had a stable relationship. I know you think of yourself as a mature eighteen, but emotion, at any age, can be very *im*mature, and you have everything to lose. Your youth and carefreeness is an asset you only value when it's lost. And I can assure you I've known very old and jaded women of twenty.'

'So have I,' Jill agreed. 'I've no intention of emulating them.' She paused before adding, 'And I'm not all that keen on children, even if I were married tomorrow. You can rest assured that the pill is right for me, Gina.' She added, 'I don't have to call you Dr Gordon, do I?' Again she gave a little laugh.

'No; I feel I've known your parents for a very long while instead of this short space of time.'

'Nothing can be measured in time,' Jill said sagely. 'What are you going to put me on?'

'Minovlar ED—oestrogen and progesterone.'

'The latter are familiar words to me,' said Jill. 'I hear a collection of names when Daddy and Adrian are having a confab and think no one hears them. Funny— I've talked of Daddy and Mummy to you today, when mostly I call them by their Christian names. Must be a dividing line where I'm conscious of their authority and my defects, perhaps. Or possible defects.'

'Never cheapen yourself, Jill; that way you'll never let them down. I'm sure they're splendid people. I consider myself very fortunate to be among you all.'

'And I consider myself very fortunate to have you to confide in.' Jill spoke with an honest appreciation.

A little shudder went over Gina as she contemplated the girl before her. Her boldness was tempered with sensitivity, and while she appeared to be concerned about all the sexist ideas, she still retained some old-fashioned values. The thought of Malcolm obtruded. It registered that Jill had used the words, 'a crush', thus facing facts and not talking in terms of love. Gina asked quietly, 'I take it you have no objection to marriage?'

Jill raised her eyebrows and looked surprised. 'Good heavens, no! But I see no reason why I should change my name, and I'll never be the good little wife who does all the chores. *If* I have children, then *he* can change the nappies too.'

There was a short silence before Gina exclaimed, 'I don't see why you need make an issue of it, when most people share the work.'

Jill's face flushed. 'But they don't all take it for granted. That's what annoys me.'

Gina smiled. 'Wait until you're a wife.'

The retort came with a certain fierceness and indiscretion. '*You* wait too, Dr Gordon!' The echo had hardly died away before Jill looked confused and apologetic. 'I'd no right to say that. My parents would be horrified,' she added frankly. 'Forgive me.'

'I'm glad you value your parents' opinion,' Gina said quietly, recognising that Jill had obviously not noticed her wedding-ring. 'You won't go far wrong if you follow their example. In the last analysis happiness is the greatest blessing, no matter what the formula used.'

Gina conveyed that the consultation was over. She wrote out a prescription which Jill took a little tentatively.

'You've been very tolerant,' she said appreciatively. 'I guess I'm a bit mixed up when it comes to it.'

'Without work,' Gina said gently, 'life can be very meaningless. Make up your mind what you really want to do.' She added, 'And don't forget that I'm here.'

'Oh,' came the earnest reply, 'I won't. . .and thank you.'

Gina felt suddenly uneasy. This was Hugh's and Anne's daughter, and although she herself had known the family such a short while, she felt involved and part of it. She didn't like the fact that she was instrumental in keeping a secret from them—a secret which would naturally distress them. When Jill had gone, Gina sought Adrian out. He had a few minutes' break and looked at her, eyebrows raised, his gaze questioning as she came quickly into his room.

'Trouble?' he asked briefly.

She outlined the situation and sat down naturally in the patients' chair. 'I feel inadequate. But what else could I do? If I refused——'

He pursed his lips and shook his head. 'That would have been fatal. At least the problem is now in the open.' His eyes were disconcerting. 'Nothing will stop two people if they want to sleep together.'

The words echoed significantly into the sudden silence. In that moment it seemed fantastic that she and Adrian were talking in this intimate fashion, nevertheless the words hung between them, demanding a comment from her.

'Our profession revolves around sex,' she said, noticing that he stared at her unblinkingly as he made a little expressive sound.

'*Life* revolves around it,' he said factually.

Gina studied him and, again, could not escape the question: Had he slept with any other woman, or with Erin, during their parting? He was a virile, passionate man, but he sat there immobile, his features relaxed as though he were talking to a pleasant friend.

She suddenly felt a little nervous and said jerkily, 'I'm relieved that you agree with my handling of the situation.'

'More than agree. But I understand your reactions, and with Hugh and Anne involved it isn't simple. One can only hope that Jill meets someone with whom she can have a stable relationship.'

The words fell between them and they looked at

each other with a certain challenge. Gina lifted her head in a gesture almost of defiance as she said, 'Since her elders fail to achieve that blissful state, it's asking a great deal for her to do so.'

His eyes darkened and met hers so deliberately that she lowered her gaze as he said, 'Nevertheless there are periods of stability even in the most turbulent relationships. Some people manage to achieve harmony for a lifetime.' A touch of bitterness sharpened his voice. 'They're singularly fortunate.' Then, as though he had no intention of continuing the conversation, he added, 'Now I must get back to work. . . Thank you for putting me in the picture and for handling the case so well.'

Gina felt dismissed and a little intimidated. She got to her feet, as he did to his, and they stood facing each other for a second before she hurried to the door, said, 'Thank you,' and was gone.

She almost bumped into Hugh on her way into the hall.

'Where's the fire?' he asked comically. He shot her an enquiring glance. 'Everything all right?'

They were both at that moment thinking of Jill, although Gina knew that Hugh would not mention her visit.

'Fine,' she said cheerfully.

He smiled. 'It's good to have you here,' he said encouragingly, and went on his way.

It was at the end of early evening surgery the following Wednesday that Adrian said to Gina, 'You'll want to get away. . .you're having dinner with Malcolm.'

She stared at him, amazed. 'Good heavens—fancy your remembering!'

'I remember how mesmerised he was when he met you and lost no time in inviting you out!'

Gina laughed, slightly embarrassed. 'As I told you—I liked him.'

'Justifiably—he's a good chap. No pretence.'

Gina shook her head and smiled. 'Coming from you that's praise indeed.'

He stiffened slightly. 'Your memory of me is hardly flattering, I notice.'

'I meant that you don't lavish praise indiscriminately. Nothing wrong with that.'

'Thank you. Perhaps I'm intrigued.' He looked at her very directly. 'After all, you *are* my ex-wife.'

She shrank from the bold assertion. 'I don't see that has anything to do with it.' Her tone was firm.

'It's a fact nevertheless.'

They faced each other a little stormily, and a few seconds later she left.

Gina didn't pretend as she showered and dressed that evening, choosing a slim powder-blue dress that moulded her figure and gave her an elegance which did not destroy her natural air of youthfulness, or emphasise any hard sophistication. She was excited, and it showed in her bright eyes and expression of eager anticipation. She felt that she knew this man she was meeting only for the second time, and Adrian's praise of him gave an element of security. For those moments when she walked the short distance to the Cotswold House Hotel, which stood prominently in the High Street, she forgot being a doctor and that she was off duty; she was suddenly free, full of anticipation and in a mood to enjoy every moment of the evening. As she went into the hotel—dating back to the seventeenth century—with its impressive entrance hall and original spiral staircase, Malcolm immediately appeared to welcome her. They had agreed to meet at seven and it was exactly two minutes past.

'I've been terrified that someone would go into labour and you'd have to cancel.' He had an air of expectant enjoyment as though a party were about to begin. His blue eyes met hers with frank admiration that deepened to a serious intensity, as he murmured, 'You look very beautiful.' And the words didn't sound banal or effusive. They quickened her heartbeat, and pleasure built up as she felt the stimulation of his personality.

'Thank you.'

His gaze didn't leave her face. 'I've got a window table,' he said as they went into the restaurant, 'so that we can look over the garden.' He stroked his tie a trifle nervously just for a split second as the head waiter came forward to greet them on their way through the pink and green room, where floor-to-ceiling windows gave light and air, while impressive pillars increased the suggestion of space.

As they sat down Gina noticed that a bottle of champagne was on ice at the table.

'This is a delightful place,' she said warmly.

'It's been restored to its original splendour,' Malcolm explained. 'Mellow stone walls and clipped yew hedges adorn the old-world garden. I suppose there must be one and a quarter acres—a mass of colour from now on.' He held her gaze and smiled. 'I don't want to talk about the hotel, but you,' he said abruptly. 'Now that you're here, I can't quite believe it.' Still his gaze held hers, his eyes watching her intently.

'But,' Gina said wonderingly, 'you don't *know* me.'

He shook his head and his expression grew solemn. 'I've known you all my life.'

'But——'

He interrupted her. 'In my imagination you've always been there. It's been a matter of finding you.' And although he spoke solemnly, there was a note of brightness in his expression.

Gina found herself comparing him with Adrian. Suppose she had married a man like Malcolm? He was, she felt instinctively, a simpler, less complicated man than Adrian.

'I think,' she said softly, 'you're allowing your imagination to run riot.'

'At least you're not denigrating me by ridicule. . . Now,' he looked at the wine waiter who hovered, 'I think it's time we had some champagne. I had a taxi here and shall get one back,' he added, 'so there isn't a driving problem.'

'It was kind of you to offer to pick me up,' she said, remembering, 'but I'm only a stone's throw away, as I told you.' She smiled. 'You obviously have a stand-in tonight.'

'Yes,' he said blithely, 'I'm off the hook. My partner has taken over. . . I'm glad you've joined Hugh and Adrian. Speaking on a purely businesslike footing. They needed you—they're a fine team. We're all excellent friends. And from my point of view your coming has changed the world.' He spoke with a quiet conviction.

She said impetuously, 'Listen, Malcolm; you don't know me, as I've already said.'

'I don't have to know you to love you,' he said simply, and looked into her eyes as a man begging for response. 'I wouldn't have believed any of this had it not happened to me. I'm in love with you, Gina. It happened like a star shooting across the sky, and as swiftly. . . I've no intention of pretending. I'm sure others noticed it—in fact I guarantee that Adrian did.'

Gina reminded herself that she was not supposed to know Adrian, and shrugged. 'I wouldn't hazard a guess.'

'You'll find that Adrian is a very perceptive man. . . I can't quite believe you're real,' he added swiftly. 'I've been waiting for this minute from the moment I understood about love.' He spoke so naturally and was so at ease as the moments passed that Gina was beguiled by his personality and drawn to him unwittingly.

She said swiftly, meeting his gaze, 'I've been divorced.'

His expression did not change as he commented, 'I'm not asking for the past, but the future. Life for us begins now.'

She panicked slightly. He was persuasive, so convincing that it was impossible to doubt his sincerity.

'I can't give you any encouragement,' she insisted.

'Tell me just one thing,' he spoke seriously.

'If I can.'

'You're not in love with anyone else?'

Gina's firm resolute, 'No,' reassured him to the point of gratitude.

'Then nothing else matters.' He relaxed. 'Now what are we going to have to eat?'

He was, she thought, an intriguing man. So frank, direct and yet with an underlying romanticism she could not ignore.

'The fresh salmon,' she said immediately as she handed back the menu to the waiter.

Malcolm nodded and joined her, with avocado to start.

They talked naturally throughout the meal, going from one subject to another, with always the awareness of his intense interest in her as a woman, his gaze deepening and seldom leaving her face, his blue eyes expressive of the love that was obvious. There were moments when Gina felt nervous and looked around her without seeing, inevitably drawn back by the steadiness of a look more eloquent than words. By the time they were about to leave, he said, 'I'll walk with you to your flat and come back for my taxi. I've only to telephone.'

She did not try to dissuade him. The evening had been a success, and she liked this man who made love to her with every gesture and intonation. It was a new experience and a refreshing change after the barrenness of her recent sexless life.

Back at the flat she said, 'Come in for a little brandy?' The words were spontaneous.

He accepted with obvious pleasure and they went into her sitting-room, from which the Market Hall was visible in the fading light, speared with the deep pink of the afterglow which lay over the ancient town like a vast sea of colour.

'This is charming,' said Malcolm as he looked around him.

'The owners spent a great deal of money here,' Gina explained. 'I wish I could have a real fire. . .' She crossed to the drinks tray and looked back at him. 'Would you?'

It struck her afresh that she might have known this man years instead of hours.

As they moved past each other, he put out his hands and clasped both hers.

'Gina?' His eyes met hers pleadingly and with passion. 'Marry me. I love you so much, and time doesn't count.'

Gently, and almost before she had time to realise what was happening, his arms went around her and his lips met hers.

CHAPTER THREE

MALCOLM'S kiss was penetrating and deep, and for a second Gina came near to responding before drawing back, a sensation of near-guilt touching her. She was not in the habit of surrendering to a man she hardly knew, and with a degree of annoyance she heard the echo of Adrian's words about her dining with strangers.

'Time,' she said firmly, 'counts to me.'

He said quickly, stepping back a pace, 'I'd no right to——' He stopped, his expression half apologetic and half appealing. 'I'm serious, Gina. I can't pretend.'

'Neither can I.' Her voice was gentler. She knew he would not attempt to kiss her again.

'I'm sorry,' he apologised, 'but I must make you realise how serious I am.'

She studied his solemn face. The idea of a stable marriage and children suddenly appealed, and she dwelt on the possibility. Malcolm was different from the men she had, thus far, met and dismissed. His personality intrigued her with its frankness and honesty.

'We all talk about love at first sight,' she said, trying to be realistic.

'Ridiculingly!' he exclaimed with annoyance. 'Always rejecting it!'

That, Gina thought, was true.

The silence was deep; it reduced them to a sudden tension that mounted until he exclaimed, 'I shan't change. Just so long as you *believe* me.'

She knew that she did; sincerity was etched on his pleasant features.

'I do,' she admitted, 'but that doesn't embrace encouragement.'

'Neither does it mean defeat,' he retorted hopefully, and poured out their drinks with an air of confidence.

Thoughts chased through Gina's head as Malcolm raised his glass.

'To the future,' he said, his eyes meeting hers.

'You don't even know the past,' she suggested with sudden anxiety. 'I'm divorced, Malcolm—as I told you.'

He stared at her for a second while he absorbed the fact, then said seriously, 'I'm asking for the future, not the past. Tell me as much or as little as you wish. I haven't been celibate; neither have I ever been a philanderer.'

She sipped her brandy and said, 'It was an amicable parting with no one else involved.'

He nodded his understanding and changed the subject.

Gina asked herself if her silence about Adrian was a form of cheating, and decided that she was merely taking Malcolm at his word, and that it would be betraying her pact with Adrian to explain further.

They talked naturally, exchanging confidences about their respective families. Every now and then a momentary silence fell, emotion flowing from Malcolm as he looked at her with unmistakable longing. She wanted to respond, and there were seconds when her heartbeats quickened and an indefinable yearning surged over her. It was, she knew, a reaction against her lonely state, and she faced the fact that desire could be dangerous.

The light faded from the sky and a blue darkness fell over the ancient town, with William Grevel's house standing out. Dating back to 1380, it was one of the first to have actual chimneys instead of just holes in the roof. William Grevel had been among the most influential woolmen, and was honoured on his memorial brass in the church as 'the flower of the wool merchants of all England'.

'I must show you Campden,' Malcolm said suddenly. 'It's steeped in history and I'd like to feel that you love it as I do. It was already established in the seventh century.' His mouth twisted into a wry smile. 'Oh, Gina—that I've been driven to talk about the town, when all I want to do is to talk about us!' He added with a sigh a short time later, 'And now I must go.'

She didn't deter him. A sudden awkwardness had crept between them and conversation had become difficult. He got to his feet and she saw him to the door.

'Thank you for this evening,' she said politely.

He looked down at her with great earnestness. 'I shall ask you every month to marry me,' he warned her.

'I believe in living one day at a time,' she commented.

'I want tomorrow.' His voice was serious. 'And your friendship in the meantime.'

The strain eased between them as she said sincerely, 'The friendship I *can* give you.' Even in that short while she knew she could trust the man standing before her whose eyes betrayed the love he had declared.

He picked up her hand and kissed it, leaving without another word.

The telephone rang as she shut the front door.

Adrian's voice startled her. He spoke quickly and there was anxiety in his voice. 'Are you alone?'

'Yes.' She was slightly irritated; what had that to do with him?

'If I collect you would you help me out with a midder that's started three weeks early? The nurse can't get there until the morning and the husband's frantic.'

Immediately Gina said, 'Of course.'

'I'll be with you in minutes,' he said urgently, and put the receiver down.

Gina just had time to hurry out of her dress into a practical blouse and skirt over which she donned a white coat, before Adrian was at the door. They went out to the car together and up the High Street as he explained, 'It's off the Hidcote Bartrim road and you'd have taken time to find it. . . Sorry to crash into the evening like this.'

'We're doctors,' she said simply, and thought, even in that second, how vastly different he was from Malcolm, with a challenge in his personality which aroused faintly antagonistic reactions, without detracting from his charm. He was, she thought, a far more dangerous type emotionally but, she argued, she would always be ready to resist his forcefulness.

There was a deep silence in the car while Adrian drove as quickly as was legally possible, ultimately arriving at a converted farmhouse where a distracted young husband flung open the door and exclaimed, 'Thank God you're here!'

'I've brought Dr Gordon with me,' Adrian explained

as they all hurried up the stairs to where Una Lindsey was in precipitate labour, in which all the stages followed one another very quickly. Adrian just had time to support the head as the child was born. 'A girl,' he said brightly, 'a sister for Andrew'—the son who was two. The explusion of the placenta followed quickly and, when the cord was cut, Gina took the baby to attend to.

Martin Lindsey held his wife's hand and looked at her adoringly. She was a fair-haired, fair-skinned girl of twenty-four who had come through the ordeal with great courage.

When, a short while later, Adrian placed the child in her arms, his gaze met and held Gina's for a second. What difference would it have made had *they* had a child? They were aware of the intimacy of the situation and looked away from each other as a wave of emotion surged between them, the obvious love and happiness that bound the parents holding up a mirror from which they both retreated.

'What name are you going to——?' Gina began.

Una Lindsey cut in, 'Clare.' She held the baby more closely, looking up at her husband, her eyes starry. 'We're so lucky. . .'

A little later Adrian and Gina left the house. Gina said as they drove away, 'No question about their happiness.'

Adrian quickened speed. 'No.'

When they reached her flat she asked, 'Would you like a cup of coffee?'

To her surprise, he said without hesitation, 'And a spot of brandy. I'd like that very much if it's not too late for you.'

'I always feel exhilarated after a birth,' she replied.

'The most exciting and depressing of a doctor's tasks,' he added.

'You mean when it's a single parent who'd hoped to be married?'

'Exactly.'

They went into the flat and he followed her into the kitchen—small unit-fitted, in white and blue.

'Well,' he said, 'we've come through our first test.'

'Test?' She turned as she was filling the kettle.

'Working on a case together. You were splendid.'

She switched on the power. 'Thank you.' She put out the cups. 'It will have to be instant,' she murmured. 'I don't bother with a percolator.'

'You always made excellent coffee.'

'One is apt to cut corners when one's alone.'

'How true.'

She was conscious of his standing there watching her, and when she had made the coffee he took the two cups into the adjoining sitting-room and glanced at the drinks tray.

'Help yourself,' Gina said easily. 'Not for me.'

'What a dull way for you to end an evening—with your ex-husband.'

'Work is never dull,' she said deliberately.

'I get the point; this is all part of work.'

'Quite pleasant, nevertheless.'

An unspoken question lay between them, and it came out jerkily a few moments later when they were both settled in their respective chairs, and Adrian had put his glass down after having sipped his brandy. It struck Gina as ironical that Malcolm had been doing the same, in the same chair, such a short while before.

'Did you have a good evening?' Adrian asked finally.
'Very enjoyable.'

They looked at each other warily. She had no
intention of satisfying his curiosity. Her evening with
Malcolm had nothing to do with him.

Still holding her gaze, he said, 'I almost expected
him to ask you to marry him.' The suggestion came
lightly, but with a touch of enquiry behind it. She knew
that he was making a statement instead of daring to
ask a question.

For a reason Gina couldn't have explained she said
boldly, 'He *did* ask me to marry him. Your intuition
was right.'

Adrian's cup rattled down on his saucer and he put
both down on the side-table, looking astounded. 'When
it comes to it,' he admitted, 'I didn't expect to be *so*
exact.' His eyebrows raised and his eyes widened, as
he added, 'Have I to wish you happiness?'

The room was very silent; an almost warring element
crept into the atmosphere. Gina didn't want to be
questioned, least of all by Adrian, but she allowed
emotion to subside as she said smoothly, 'You can wish
me happiness by all means, but not because I'm going
to rush into marriage with a man I hardly know.'

'I transgress,' Adrian said half apologetically. 'I have
no right to pry.'

She relaxed. 'To fail once is painful,' she said quietly,
'to do so twice would be fatal to me.'

'And to me,' he agreed.

She thought of Malcolm in that moment, warming to
the memory of his declaration and the fact that he was
a man with whom one could be secure, never doubting.
The memory of his kiss stirred her and she wondered,

her cheeks flushing, what would have happened had she responded, and what Adrian would say were she to tell him. Faint irritation mounted. Why even think of that? Her actions had nothing whatsoever to do with him.

'I take it,' she said, changing the subject abruptly, 'that you have domestic help?'

'Daily; a housekeeper-cum-cook when I need her. I eat out quite a bit. And you?'

'Just a daily. She went with the flat, as it were.' She spoke formally, and he was aware of the fact that the introduction of Malcolm's name had changed the atmosphere.

He finished his drink. There was a coldness in his expression as he said, 'It's time I left you in peace. I've intruded enough for one evening.' He got to his feet, all intimacy falling away. 'Thank you for your help.' The words had a clipped appreciation which Gina was quick to notice. She found that she had nothing to say and was suddenly self-conscious as she led the way to the door.

'Goodnight, Gina,' he said crisply. His expression was inscrutable as he left without a backward glance.

She told herself as she went back into the sitting-room that their relationship would be harmonious just so long as they kept to professional matters. Nothing had changed between them. The thought of Malcolm obtruded. His easy manner was in such direct contrast, and she could not help being flattered by his love. She rejected the word 'flattered' as being facile and substituted—'honoured', because he was obviously a man of substance whose loyalty and sincerity were sacrosanct.

It would be very easy to be influenced by his persist-
ence. She longed for the excitement of loving, the
involvement, and shrank from her present sterile state.
Malcolm, she told herself, had stirred her from her
emotional complacency and she doubted if she would
be able to return to it.

She went to bed deciding that she had been very
foolish to join forces with Hugh Fawcett, since Adrian
was a partner, and that in future she would be distant
and merely professionally involved. It had been stupid
to invite Adrian in for a coffee, and she was certainly
not going to encourage him to take any interest in her
personal affairs. On the other hand, fairness intruded:
Malcolm's behaviour *was* a subject for controversy.

The next month passed uneventfully. Gina gave
everything to the practice and did not draw Adrian into
her private life at any level. They were friendly col-
leagues who had no contact at the end of the day. They
met at Hugh's and Anne's gatherings, and Malcolm
was always there, attentive, obviously in love, but
never intrusive. Jill said to Gina one evening when
Gina, Malcolm and Adrian were having supper at Mill
Lodge, 'Are you going to marry Malcolm?' She added
hastily, 'Or am I speaking out of turn?' She went on,
'If he looked at me as he looks at you, I'd faint with
emotion! Are you really as cool as you seem?'

'Which question shall I answer first?' Gina tried not
to show her irritation.

'I've annoyed you. . . Sorry. I never mean to be
rude.'

Malcolm overheard the conversation and Adrian was
close by, waiting for Gina's answer.

It came smoothly, but without obvious annoyance.

'You *are* speaking out of turn!' She gave a little nervous laugh, aware of Adrian's disturbing gaze upon her in almost intimate enquiry.

Gina looked at the distressed woman sitting opposite her. She was thirty-eight, but looked fifty. She was the last patient after a heavy surgery.

'I'm new here,' she said disconsolately. 'My husband's firm moved from Windsor and he couldn't afford to lose his job.'

'And you've been used to a male doctor.'

Colour mounted Mrs Young's face as she said, 'Yes; I've had a Dr Basil Waters for my children. . . I've got *four* and I'm pregnant again. We can't *afford* them, even if I could cope.' Her voice broke.

Rita Young was a little sparrow of a woman, whose voice seemed to come from the back of her throat and break on the point of impact. 'And before you say anything, Doctor, I can't take the pill. I've tried all sorts, and I have nothing but periods with the other methods.' There was despair in the utterance.

Gina said immediately. 'The condom?'

Colour rose in the pale face. 'My husband won't. . . I'm desperate. We haven't the *money*. With two children we could have lived reasonably, but with five. . . We're not Catholics, so religion isn't the problem.' She sighed. 'And God knows I've persevered with everything.' Again colour rose in her cheeks. 'I've had two miscarriages as well. I've no strength any more.'

'What do you weigh?'

'Barely seven stone.' She brushed aside a tear and straightened her shoulders.

Gina said gently, 'We can help you, Mrs Young.

That's what we're here for. We'll need to give you a thorough check-up, but I think this is a case for sterilisation. We can't force your husband to use a condom——'

'Dr Waters wouldn't agree to sterilisation. I'm healthy, you see,' came the ironic comment. The voice broke. 'But I don't feel it, Doctor; and all the work. . .' A glazed look came into her eyes. 'Sometimes I feel suicidal, and it isn't as though my husband doesn't love me or the children——'

Gina wanted to explode. 'But——' she began, and stopped. Why question the one straw of hope and happiness to which this poor wretched woman clung?

'He's good in so many ways and often helps, but he's got this—this revulsion against condoms; even more so since the AIDS business. I don't want you to think he's just. . .' The word faded away.

'I understand,' Gina said, adding, 'it's not an uncommon reaction.'

Mrs Young cupped her hands over her face and a sob rose in her throat. 'Thank you,' she whispered brokenly. 'I was so afraid of coming here today. Dr Waters knew me.' She recovered, dried her eyes, apologised.

'I'd like Dr Marland to see you,' Gina said encouragingly. 'If we think that your life and future are at risk with another pregnancy, then we shall terminate and sterilise at the same time. Now let me have a look at you.'

Mrs Young sat there staring, hope stirring in her frail tormented body and mind.

She was, Gina judged, in no fit state to carry a child

to term. Her blood-pressure was high; she was under-nourished and underweight, even allowing for the pregnancy where loss so often occurred.

'You've been so kind,' came the faltering words when the examination was over. 'I'm not making a fuss—really I'm not. I love children, but——'

'You haven't the strength to look after, or bear, any more,' Gina said firmly, and she knew she would fight Adrian if he didn't agree with her verdict. 'When did you last see Dr Waters?' she asked.

'Nearly a month ago. What with the moving and transferring to you. . .'

'I think his opinion would be very different now.'

Mrs Young relaxed slightly. Then she asked fearfully, 'What's Dr Marland like?'

'Very understanding.' She added, 'Could you come in tomorrow if he can see you?'

'Yes,' came the immediate reply. 'My mother is staying with me and will look after the chiildren.'

Gina flicked down the intercom and spoke to Mrs Greyson. The only time Dr Marland was free was at twelve-thirty. The appointment was made.

'You'll be there?' It was an anxious sound. 'You'll support me and I won't feel so alone.'

Gina gave the assurance.

Later that day, Adrian and Gina had a few minutes alone.

'I understand I've got a patient of yours to see tomorrow,' he said, looking at her directly.

She gave him the details, finishing with, 'I'd like to be with you when you see Mrs Young, if you've no objection.'

'On the contrary. I can well imagine the state of the

woman's mind, and anything that gives her confidence. . . You're very adamant about this case.'

She didn't pretend, and her voice was firm as she said, 'I feel strongly about it, but I've got to have another opinion.'

'On the principle that no termination can take place without the consent of two doctors.'

'Yes.'

'And if I disagree?' He shot the question at her.

His gaze met hers in faint challenge.

'Yours is the superior opinion,' she conceded, 'but I'd ask for Malcolm to be called in.'

His expression hardened. 'No one ever thwarts you, in fact.'

'Is that a judgement?' Her voice was clipped.

'No—an assessment, made with some validity.' His eyes darkened and looked at her with disarming challenge.

Gina didn't rise to it. All she said was, 'We'll take the case on its merits. I know equally that you're a humanitarian at heart.'

He smiled, a slow reflective smile. 'You're also a tactician, Gina. I shall look forward to Mrs Young's case.

There was no question of Adrian opposing Gina's verdict.

'We'll make arrangements, Mrs Young, for you to be admitted,' he said confidently, 'and you'll have no more worries. It's essential that this is done as quickly as possible.' He added with understanding, 'Can you arrange your domestic affairs to allow for this?'

Mrs Young told him, flashing a glance at Gina as she

did so, that her mother would help out, and that she herself wouldn't have survived without her mother's help. As the mother was a widow it was simple for her to be available. She added poignantly, 'One day I hope I'll be able to make up to her for all her goodness to me. . . Thank you, Dr Marland, and you, Dr Gordon, for helping me.' And even as the last word died away she slid from her chair to the floor in a dead faint.

Together Adrian and Gina got her to the examining couch and brought her round. Her face was parchment and her dark eyes wide and appealing, as she said in a breath, 'I'm so *sorry*.'

When a little later she had gone, Mrs Greyson brought in coffee and sandwiches and put the tray on Adrian's desk.

'Mrs Fawcett sent you these. She heard you were working almost through lunchtime.'

'Bless her,' said Gina.

'You've got fifteen minutes,' came the practical comment. 'You, Dr Marland, have to be at the hospital to see the Caesarean baby——'

'Ah, Mrs Wilkins,' he said immediately.

'Yes; and you, Dr Gordon——'

'I know,' Gina cut in, 'I've got a Mrs Greenway. Pregnancy check-up.'

Irene Greyson smiled. Dr Gordon seemed to remember every appointment without consulting her day-book. She reached the door. 'Nurse Lane's had one of those mornings; a nose-bleed, and she had to alert Dr Fawcett for an appendix case. . .never a dull moment!'

Adrian said, when he and Gina were alone, 'We're lucky in our staff.'

Gina was pouring out the coffee and she nodded her agreement as she handed him his cup. 'Bless Anne too; she thinks of everything, and her sandwiches are an art in themselves.' She stopped, her expression changing. 'I didn't expect you to back me up quite so readily over Mrs Young. . . Thank you.'

'You were right. It was a simple case really. A life ruined and those of four children, or a chance to adjust and consolidate a family. Your assessment was correct. Women allergic to the pill and to intra-uterine devices are, fortunately, in the minority, but one can't condemn them to further misery for that reason. One's opinion of the husband is better not discussed. And to have made an issue of it would have jeopardised the relationship further. She's obviously still in love with him.'

The words fell between them with a strange irony. They had been in love and here they were, friendly strangers, the bond of medicine their only link.

Gina said quietly, avoiding Adrian's gaze, 'I'm sure she felt that she'd failed him by her reactions to birth control, which evened out the blame.'

'Do we ever know the truth of marriage?' he asked, and looked at her with deep enquiry.

The silence that fell between them was suddenly full of emotion.

'Do we ever know ourselves, let alone marriage?' she replied.

He looked at her with a dark, lingering tension. 'I only know that I've enjoyed working with you, Gina.' He drained his coffee-cup and got to his feet.

Gina followed and they met in the centre of the room, their arms touching, their eyes meeting, almost startled as they were both aware of the physical contact.

He said, still holding her gaze, 'You said in the beginning that you'd think about having dinner with me when we'd worked together for a while. Have I qualified for the honour?'

She moved a pace away from him, her heart beating erractically. Accepting, she felt, would be like crossing a dangerous bridge. But she answered, 'I think Mrs Young put the seal on our relationship.'

'Then that means "yes".' He continued to look at her intently. 'But how about making it supper? I'd like to talk without interruption.' There was significance in his words. 'I can arrange for my Mrs Mercer to——'

She interrupted him, without realising her impulsiveness. 'Let me take care of it. . .we don't have to stand on ceremony.'

'You mean my coming to you?'

The words fell between them and for a second they both lowered their gaze.

'Yes.'

Gina knew she had taken a momentous step, but in that moment emotion was stronger than reason.

CHAPTER FOUR

GINA awakened a few mornings later with a feeling of trepidation. Adrian was coming to supper that evening, and she was apprehensive as she dwelt on the fact. This was the last thing she had originally intended, and she criticised herself for her impulsiveness. However, by the time he arrived she had regained her confidence and greeted him with a pleasant friendliness to which he responded. She noticed how smart he looked in his cream jacket, navy trousers and blue shirt, while, in turn, he admired her primrose and white polka-dot dress with its scarf-like neckline. As she stood at the door to welcome him the June sun formed a halo around her head, shading her hair to gold. The evening was warm, and a soft breeze came in through the open windows as they went into the flat.

'How about a glass of chilled white wine?' she asked. 'I've got some Vouvray. . . We can eat when we like. It's a buffet, so it's all ready.'

'I'd love a glass of wine,' he answered approvingly, and followed her into the kitchen without further comment as she took the bottle from the fridge. He noticed the corkscrew on its hook and reached out for it. Their gaze met for a fraction of a second and in a few minutes they were settled in the sitting-room, raising their respective glasses. Adrian had taken over, and the word 'divorce' lay between them significantly.

A sudden silence fell and Gina could not think of anything to say, plunging finally into banality.

'You missed lunch today.'

'So the grapevine informed you, no doubt,' he said. 'I'd hate to try to keep anything from our staff!'

'It's their job to be in the know.' She relaxed slightly; so long as they kept to practice matters she would be at ease. It registered that Adrian did not tell her why he had forgone his lunch, but changed the subject by mentioning lightly that Malcolm had done a Caesar on Mrs Morby, but, even so, couldn't save the child.

They looked at each other, both aware that they were making conversation despite the gravity of his last statement.

'You look younger than you did when we were married,' he said abruptly.

Gina made a contradictory gesture and exclaimed, 'I don't take flattery seriously.'

He studied her intently. 'And if you've ever known anything at all about me, you should realise that it's not an indulgence of mine.'

She wanted to lower her gaze from his, but was incapable of escaping from its power. 'Then it would be ungracious of me to suggest that freedom obviously suits me.'

'I don't dispute that.' His deep voice reminded her that it had always been a feature she had particularly admired.

'I'm intrigued,' she said immediately.

'But that doesn't imply that I see your freedom as permanent. I'm too well aware of Malcolm for that.'

'Reverting to your original remark, I don't think *you* have changed. . . Suppose we talk about you?' She noticed that he immediately looked away from her and concentrated on his drink.

'I'm a very dull subject,' he exclaimed dismissively. 'It's amazing how well you've settled into the practice. Hugh is delighted; so am I.'

She felt irritated because it was obvious that he had no intention of discussing his life, or even his reactions. There had always been unknown depths in him which on many occasions had distanced him from her, and the fact was manifesting itself even now. His presence disturbed her, and she could not ignore the strength of his personality, which seemed a challenge. She was acutely conscious of him sitting there, tall, long-limbed and seemingly at ease. His gaze was perturbing and inescapable, and it lingered on hers in silent admiration.

'Shall we eat?' she said as she put down her empty glass.

Adrian agreed readily, and they went through into the dining-room.

The familiarity of the lace tablecloth on which the buffet was arranged caused him to flash her a glance of remembrance which stirred her. It had been used on so many festive occasions and was a treasured family possession. Gina did not pretend that she had not used it deliberately.

'It all looks very attractive,' he said with genuine appraisal. 'I notice you haven't forgotten my taste in food.' He indicated the smoked salmon.

'Habit dies hard,' she commented.

'Some famous person once said that habit was stronger than emotion.' He watched her intently.

'I should think that would depend on the time factor.'

He nodded, and ate heartily of the dishes set before him, ending with peaches in brandy and Cointreau.

'A banquet,' he said appreciatively. 'Thank you, Gina. I've enjoyed every mouthful.'

The past rushed back and they both knew it. When they returned to the sitting-room he took her in his arms as though it was an inevitable sequel as he said, 'You're very lovely, Gina.'

His touch roused her; desire flooded back and her lips parted beneath his in a long passionate kiss, after which their eyes met, a question was mutely asked and answered, and they went into the adjoining bedroom, emotion rising while they clung together, undressed each other lingeringly and moved towards the bed. No words were spoken; his body pressed against hers, the sensuality of flesh against flesh leading them to that final ecstasy when they cried out, and they lay close and still, her head on his shoulder, his lips against her forehead, the silence deep and significant; a silence which Gina wanted Adrian to break and which made her uneasy. What was he thinking? What did he feel, now that rapture was spent and satiated? If they could be here like this, why couldn't they have remained married? What impulse had made her surrender so easily, so naturally? Yet familiarity had not lessened the ecstasy of the act; his touch had not lost its magic because of the time lapse. She did not deceive herself: she had wanted him even when they had sat drinking their wine. It was a strange and disturbing sensation which she had pretended she was imagining, making her feel embarrassed.

And now here she was, lying with his arms around her, tightening for a second as he whispered her name. 'Gina'—not 'darling'. Yet what did she want him to say? This was sexual fulfilment, not love, and to pretend would be self-deception. The memory of the past stirred her, giving this moment a familiarity that touched poignancy. Now her ex-husband was her lover. The moment his lips touched hers, passion had usurped all other emotion, and the result was inevitable as it had been since the morning he had said to her, 'Welcome, Dr Gordon. I hope you'll be very happy here.'

Every now and then his body pressed closer to hers and his arms tightened, conveying that it was enough that they were there together.

When it was time for him to go, she slid into a satin housecoat and sat on the edge of the bed while he dressed. There was no embarrassment. She noticed the way he flicked his tie into place, without looking in the mirror. How much practice had he had during their parting? Who else had lain in his arms?

Finally he held her gently and with tenderness.

'It's been a perfect evening,' he said in a voice that thrilled her. He drew her gaze to his before kissing her, and leaving.

The flat was empty; the silence oppressive. She didn't know whether she was happy or sad. If only he had talked to her, told her something of how he felt. Was this the beginning of a relationship, or one night of passion that led nowhere? Her own reactions were chaotic; emotion washed over her and she trembled as she went back into the bedroom and looked at the crumpled sheets, the dent in the pillow where his head

had lain. It was all so natural and yet fantastic. Had
she been mad? Had he intended to make love to her,
or was it as spontaneous on his part as on hers? She
knew she would never have the courage to ask him.
And so she was left wondering; in turmoil, as she
returned to the empty bed which now seemed large
and lonely.

Gina felt that the staff must know of the interlude as
she met them the following morning. It was strange,
she thought, how a single act could change both
outlook and attitude.

Adrian opened the door of Mrs Greyson's room and
paused with his hand on the knob. Gina stood there
rather like a rabbit before a stoat as his gaze flicked to
hers and he said formally, 'Good morning, Dr
Gordon. . . Mrs Greyson, will you send Mr Stokes
straight in when he arrives?' With that he went out and
shut the door.

'Brief and to the point,' Mrs Greyson remarked.

Gina was trembling. 'It's probably going to be one
of those days,' she said, and managed to laugh
hollowly.

Janet Westbury, cheeks slightly flushed, rose to the
remark. 'Dr Marland has a very busy day.'

As she spoke, and by her attitude. Gina thought of
the flowers that found their way into Adrian's room,
and how she had originally decided that Janet
Westbury was the donor.

Nurse Lane flashed a smile at Gina. 'Dr Marland has
a champion in Janet.'

Gina watched Janet Westbury's expression darken
and her body stiffen as she stood by Mrs Greyson's

desk, and felt sorry for her. There was no question about her feelings for Adrian.

'Ten minutes to surgery, Dr Gordon,' Mrs Greyson announced. 'You and Mr Fawcett are on this morning.'.

Gina passed Adrian's room on the way to her own. Her heart quickened its beat as she thought of the previous night and felt again the passion and thrill of his body pressed against her own. Would he come to see her? She listened as she sat at her desk, then heard his footsteps and, after a second, his voice asking if she had a minute.

'Just about.' She maintained control and spoke naturally, but she was thinking, You made love to me last night and yet you stand there almost as a stranger.

'I'm going to induce the Halstead baby.' He spoke quickly, his gaze seeking her approval.

She didn't want to talk about anyone's baby; she wanted to talk about *them*, but she recapped, 'Mrs Halstead is the high blood-pressure case, coming up to term.'

'A matter of days, but she's exhausted. Do you agree with me?'

'She's your patient.' Gina felt irritated.

'But I value your opinion. . . Are you all right?'

'Perfectly.' Her voice was crisp. Did he regret his impulsive behaviour the previous night?

Their eyes met and the atmosphere changed.

'Gina——' he began, his voice enticing.

At that moment the intercom went. Mrs Greyson said, 'Your first patient, Dr Gordon, and Mr Fawcett has already started.'

'Surgery,' Adrian said on a note of frustration. 'And I've got Mr Stokes at any minute. We'll talk again.'

What, Gina asked herself, had he been about to say? He went from the room without another word.

During the next fortnight they had little time to be alone. Hugh had a bad bout of summer flu, so that the practice demanded their undivided attention; nevertheless Adrian's manner held a slight reservation, and with a mixture of resentment and regret Gina decided that he had come to regard their making love as a mistake, wishing to extricate himself from the situation as delicately as possible.

It was one morning when they had a few minutes' breathing-space that his gaze met hers in an intimate, passionate look, and he was about to draw her into his arms when an urgent knock on the door preceded Nurse Lane's and Jill's entrance.

Jill cried out painfully, 'I'm so. . .sorry, but——' She crumpled up, clutching her stomach, while a tell-tale red stain appeared down her leg.

Adrian lifted her in his arms and carried her to the examining couch, Gina following, indicating to Nurse Lane to stay and attend to the patient. Gina murmured to Adrian, 'I'd like your support.'

Jill clutched Gina's hand; a little moan escaped her.

'Tell me,' Gina said gently, 'what's happened to you—why?'

Jill explained disjointedly that she hadn't taken the pill and had gone to an unexpected party where she'd had too much champagne, and awoke to find that she'd slept with a man who was almost a stranger. . .it was about six weeks ago.

Gina began her examination, finding extreme tenderness in the lower abdomen, and that, together with the internal bleeding and other symptoms, gave her the

diagnosis. She said in a breath when Adrian came
within her line of vision and Nurse Lane pulled up the
sheet, 'This is an ectopic. . . An ectopic pregnancy,'
she added to Jill.

In a normal pregnancy the fertilised egg passed down
the Fallopian tube and grew into a foetus in the wall of
the uterine cavity. In an ectopic pregnancy it failed to
do so and started to develop in another area, the most
common site being the Fallopian tube, as now.

Jill groaned in shock. She understood the
terminology.

Adrian and Gina exchanged meaning glances. Gina
said quickly, 'We must get her into the Randall—a
local nursing home—and operate immediately. If Malcolm could do it——'

Jill cried out, 'My parents——'

Both Hugh and Anne were out, and at that juncture
neither could be contacted.

Adrian alerted the Randall and sent for an ambulance; every second was vital. Malcolm, with some
manoeuvring, made himself available and arranged to
go straight to the nursing home. He would do a
laparotomy to remove the affected tube.

Jill was in so much pain and distress that only Gina's
presence registered.

'Please come. . .' she murmured.

'I'll come with you,' Gina promised, and looked at
Adrian for approval.

'I'll see to things here and trace Hugh and Anne.
Hugh's doing a hysterectomy. . .'

Jill groaned and then a word escaped her lips.
'*Mummy*. . .' In that moment she was only eighteen,

and frightened. But even then it registered that, thank God, she wouldn't be having a baby.

To Hugh and Anne the news had the impact of an earthquake. It wasn't that they had deluded themselves that Jill was 'different', but her somewhat outrageous views and attitudes seemed to preclude sexual irresponsibility. They were thankful that Malcolm had operated and acted with such speed, knowing that Jill would have to be watched carefully for a couple of days and then, if there was no infection, would be home within a week.

Now, the drama over, Adrian, Gina and Malcolm were gathered at Mill Lodge, Hugh and Anne having made their last visit to the nursing home.

Hugh looked at them. 'Thank God for you,' he said fervently.

'I'm afraid,' Adrian explained, 'that in the circumstances we had to take matters into our own hands and act on our initiative.'

Gina dragged her thoughts away from Jill for a moment as she studied Adrian. The events of the day had crashed into their intimacy, and she was haunted by the spectre of what might have been, as it was impossible to judge by his manner since the event.

Malcolm, on the other hand, no matter how professional he was called upon to be, always left her in no doubt of his feelings. It could be a look, gesture, or smile, and this occasion was no exception. When they were about to part he asked, 'Would you like to come to see *Romeo and Juliet* as the Royal Shakespeare Theatre? We can finalise it tomorrow.' They had parted from Hugh and Anne and were standing by their respective cars, Adrian just getting into his, nodding to them in turn as he said goodnight and drove off.

Gina didn't hesitate as, almost in defiance, she said she would very much like to go. The sound of Adrian's car mingled with the echo of her voice, and it seemed that he had disappeared into a different world, as though he wanted to avoid further contact with her. Another unruly thought chased through her mind: was it that after their night together he felt he had prior claim? Yet, not having established the fact, how could she be expected to make any decision on the matter? Colour rose in her cheeks as she realised that she was not the type to go to bed, even with her ex-husband without feeling that some kind of commitment was necessary. When it came to it, had she subconsciously regarded that night as a prelude to a physical bond having nothing to do with love and marriage?

'Where,' Malcolm asked wryly, 'have you been during these past seconds? You've gone from me completely.'

She managed to say quickly, 'The general confusion of the day and the juxtaposition of your suggesting *Romeo and Juliet*.'

'Ah!' He was satisfied. 'I suppose this was hardly the time to talk of the theatre, but you are very elusive.'

Gina reminded herself that she had only promised Malcolm friendship, therefore her life apart from that was her own.

Adrian, during the few minutes he and Gina were alone the following day, seemed distracted, his gaze avoiding hers, the short conversations embracing purely medical matters.

'Jill,' he said finally, 'is recovering well. So far, so

good. Hugh and Anne have been splendid. It must have been a great shock.'

'It was even to me,' Gina admitted. 'She hadn't even begun to take the pill, apparently, and the party was an unexpected affair—the kind to which she wouldn't normally go. But I suppose this is kinder than an unwanted pregnancy.' As she spoke, Gina recalled Jill's stricken face when she had talked to her earlier that morning. The bombast gone, contrition and self-loathing in its place.

'I've been such a fool, so sure of myself, prepared for any eventuality, and then before I'd even started taking the pill—this!' Jill had said. 'I shall never remember all that happened that night. It's horrible, and I feel degraded, part of everything I despise.'

Adrian looked solemn. 'I hate to see Hugh and Anne shattered.' His expression changed as he said rather awkwardly, 'I've got a letter to dictate to Mrs Greyson before I go out.' He almost mumbled, 'A busy day.'

'Aren't they all?' Gina retorted crisply, and walked towards the door, her attitude unconsciously defensive.

The silence was heavy.

'We'll make up for it,' he assured her, his gaze suddenly intent.

She threw him a doubting glance over her shoulder as she went out, angry that he had the power to annoy her, and even more annoyed that she had omitted to tell him that she was going to the theatre with Malcolm as soon as it could be arranged. Why was it, she asked herself, that in moments of tension one forgot the important details?

It was the following day after lunch that she snatched an hour to do some shopping and walked down the wide High Street, with its pronounced curve—one side much lower than the other. The July sun, miraculously bright, fell on the varying architectural styles, mostly with Cotswold stone walls and roofs, the houses having no front gardens, but many with large ones at the back which stretched either to Calf Lane or Back Ends. Gina had not seen Adrian that morning, but Malcolm had telephoned her to say that he had managed to get seats for *Romeo and Juliet* the following week and that they could have a meal at the King's Arms Hotel in Campden which specialised in early and late suppers for those who were going to Stratford to the theatre, only twelve miles away. She could see the hotel as she walked to the chemist—it was on the sunny side of the street and dated back to the sixteenth century. It had picturesque gardens and the atmosphere of yesterday.

The thought of Adrian became visual in that moment, and she lost herself in contemplation of their relationship, his inscrutability mocking the passion of their night together, when suddenly with shock, she saw him coming out of the hotel with Erin Foster.

CHAPTER FIVE

THE first shock over, Gina hesitated as to whether she should make her presence known, but decided against it and watched, concealed in a shop entrance which nevertheless gave her a view of the hotel. Her pulse had quickened and there was a sinking sensation in her stomach. So—Erin was still in the picture and doubtless the cause of Adrian's recent abstraction. She studied them intently as he looked down into Erin's upturned face, finding that she herself was trembling. She could visualise the appeal of Erin's wide-set eyes, and noticed that her lustrous dark hair was still worn upswept. She had on a floral-patterned dress and looked smart. They stood in earnest conversation until the moment of parting, when Adrian put a hand on her shoulder and then moved away. Erin watched him get into his car and, turning, went back into the hotel.

Gina forgot half her shopping and returned to Mill Lodge as quickly as possible. It was as though it represented a sanctuary where she could hide her fears and disillusionments. Yet why shouldn't Adrian and Erin have kept in touch? But why the secrecy? She decided she would not mention the events of the morning when, at the end of the day, she and Adrian met to discuss a thyroid case that had been concerning them. The treatment agreed on, they faced each other a little awkwardly, and all Gina's resolutions fell away before the challenge of his presence and the memory of his parting from Erin.

Suddenly, discretion deserting her, she said somewhat cynically, 'You've had an eventful day.'

There was a sudden silence which he broke by retorting, 'I'd hardly call it that.'

She looked at him with unnerving directness. 'I saw you with Erin this morning outside the King's Arms.'

Thunder might have rumbled through the room.

'I was going to tell you she's settling in Campden.'

Her gaze was direct and, without realising it, accusing. 'But you didn't.' She regretted the words the moment they were uttered.

He frowned, and then raised his eyebrows in a look of protest. 'What is this—an inquisition?'

Was that his way of conveying that, because they had been intimate, there was no reason why she should be privy to his personal life?

She protested, 'I expressed myself badly.'

'A habit you've evidently not lost where Erin is concerned,' he said tartly.

'Oh, don't let's make an issue of it!' she protested.

He shook his head. 'If that isn't typical of a woman——'

They faced each other stormily, behaving as though they were still husband and wife.

'And your secrecy is also typical,' she accused him.

'Can you blame me? Subconsciously, I wanted to avoid just such a scene.'

The word offended her, forcing home how badly she had handled the situation. She was mad ever to have gone to bed with him and could not accept it as having little emotional significance, whereas he, man-like, could dismiss it when it came to any serious discussion or implication. Now she felt that once again their relationship was disintegrating, leaving her tense and vulnerable.

She managed to say with emphasis, 'The last thing I want, either, is a scene.'

'Then that makes two of us,' he said, striving to introduce a placatory note. He added, his expression sombre, 'Actually, I wanted your help where Erin is concerned.'

Gina gave an amazed exclamation. '*My* help?'

'As she's about to move into a cottage near us here, she wants to become your patient.' He added hastily, 'She has friends in the district and intends eventually to get a job in Campden.'

So, Gina reflected, he had obviously kept in touch with Erin since the divorce, and she was familiar with the workings at Mill Lodge.

'If she requires a doctor, why not you?' Gina demanded.

'Because she needs, and prefers, a woman to take care of her.'

'Me!' The word was uttered in astonishment.

'Yes.'

Gina's voice was icy. 'As a doctor I have a duty to look after anyone who wishes to see me.' Was he, she asked herself, avoiding the danger of the doctor-patient relationship in the circumstances? She added, 'As your assistant I have no alternative but to agree to your request.'

He looked shocked. 'That phase,' he countered sharply, 'had not occurred to me.'

She believed him as she said, 'Obviously I'll do my

very best for her.' And in that moment all familiarity
fell away. They were two doctors talking about a
patient in an alien atmosphere of formality. She wanted
to challenge him as to why—since he was apparently
so involved in Erin's life—he had not married her, and
his cool acceptance of the situation, as though Erin's
being in the picture was the most normal advent,
irritated her. He had always adopted that attitude, and
Gina was dismayed to find that it still had the same
power to stir up resentment. He appeared to be so
blatantly honest when all the time he was infuriatingly
secretive. Pride forbade her questioning him.

'I take it,' Gina asked, 'that Erin is staying at the
King's Arms?'

'For another day or two.'

Gina persisted. 'From your description, her
cottage——'

He interrupted hastily, 'It's just off Station Road—
very near. Her friends own it and are letting her have
it furnished until she gets settled.'

That conveyed permanence. Was it possible that he
had it in mind to include Erin in the practice? But in
what capacity, since she was a medical secretary and
they were certainly not in need of one?

He might have been reading her thoughts as he
explained, 'Malcolm might be glad of her to help out.
His secretary, as you know, is leaving to get married.'

Thoughts darted in unruly fashion through Gina's
mind. The last thing she wanted was Erin in close
proximity to Malcom, thus being drawn into the circle
and no doubt becoming friendly with Hugh and Anne.
The very possibility made life untidy, and her nerves
tingled as she contemplated the near future.

The sudden silence was heavy, and Adrian broke it by saying, 'I gather you don't approve of the idea.'

Gina bristled, but managed to say smoothly, 'It has nothing to do with me. You always said what an excellent secretary Erin was——'

'Not *my* secretary——'

'I know that,' she nearly snapped, realising that they were sliding into a quarrel. 'In a hospital people are switched around.'

'Not people of Erin's calibre. She was——' He stopped, looking slightly embarrassed. 'But you won't have forgotten that she was with Mr Wingate, the orthopaedics consultant.'

'No,' Gina agreed meaningly, 'my memory doesn't fail me.'

'Nor,' he retorted cuttingly, 'your prejudices.'

Colour rose in her cheeks. 'At least you give me credit for not having any prejudices when it comes to patients,' she exclaimed tartly. 'Get Erin to ring me and I'll see her immediately.'

He lowered his gaze as he said, 'Thank you.' There was faint hesitation before he added, 'Enlist Hugh's aid if you're in any doubt about her case.' He paused before saying unguardedly, 'I'm too close to be objective.'

His words fell heavily, and Gina took them literally.

'That,' she retorted pointedly, 'is obvious, and I appreciate it.'

'I didn't make myself clear,' he explained hastily, looking awkward.

'On the contrary.' Her voice was smooth. 'But if I'm in any doubt I'll discuss the matter with Hugh.' She paused. 'You'll get all the facts from Erin herself, anyway.' It was a direct challenge, but he did not rise to it and his silence seemed a capitulation. There was nothing further to say.

Erin telephoned later that day and came to see Gina the following morning. Gina studied her without criticism as she sat down in the patients' chair. She had an air of sadness about her that shadowed her wide-set blue eyes in an expression that was unconsciously pleading for understanding. At no time had Gina disliked her as a person, but they had not been on intimate terms of friendship, just an acceptance of an acquaintanceship fostered by Erin's association with Adrian at the hospital. There was no colour in her olive skin and she sat very still—the mystery woman in the case, Gina thought, yet not one who aroused antipathy, but rather conjecture. She looked small, slim and appealing in her navy and white button-through cotton dress. What was her relationship with Adrian? Had they ever been lovers, and why had she followed him—as was reasonable to suppose—to Chipping Campden after this lapse of time? Above all, why had they not married? A tremor went over Gina's body as a thought struck her for the first time: was Erin married already and perhaps awaiting a divorce? Professional instinct killed further ruminations and Gina said encouragingly, 'Tell me what's troubling you.'

'I think I'm just run down, and now that I'm here I almost feel a fraud for worrying you.' Erin hurried on, studying Gina intently, 'It seems a very long while ago since we last met at the hospital ball.' She stopped abruptly. The occasion had coincided with the announcement of the divorce and was the last time Adrian and Gina had appeared together in public.

'A great deal has happened since then.' Gina had no intention of reminiscing. She saw the shadow that fell across Erin's face, and she looked ill at ease and apprehensive. It was obvious that she was not going to betray any emotional secrets.

'"Run down" covers a multitude of sins. Can you be more specific?' said Gina.

'Very heavy periods, no energy or appetite, and I fainted the other day—not right off, but very nearly.' Erin met Gina's contemplative gaze. 'I wanted to get settled before going into the matter, so that I can get back to work. Adrian mentioned Dr Villiers.'

How easily, Gina thought, she spoke of Adrian; without awkwardness or reticence and as though she, Gina, would accept it as being normal.

Gina became purely professional, refusing to be hampered medically by circumstances. 'Have you any emotional problems likely to affect your health?'

There was a tense silence. Erin lowered her gaze, smoothed one hand over the other and then looked at Gina with honest eyes. 'None that is new; the upheaval of moving, finding the right place——' She shook her head and didn't take the matter further.

'Why do you want me to look after you?' The question came involuntarily.

'Because I always knew that you were a good doctor; also, I prefer a woman. Do you mind?'

Gina kept her voice steady. 'Why should I?'

Erin's voice faltered. 'No reason. I'm glad that you and Adrian are friends.'

Wasn't that, Gina asked herself, a proprietorial note? Almost a possessive one?

She ignored the remark and said briefly, 'Let me

examine you.' She got to her feet and opened the door to the examining-room. 'Just leave your slip on.'

Gina's instinctive diagnosis was that Erin was suffering from a form of anaemia, which only further investigation could confirm.

'We'll get a blood test done,' she said after she had gone through the routine meticulously.

'Anaemia?' It was a statement in the form of a question.

'Quite possibly, but I don't believe in accepting what may seem to be the obvious.'

'The heavy periods are the greatest curse,' Erin told her.

Gina shut her mind against the implications of the remark and the effect upon the sexual side of things. 'Until we get the result of the blood test I'd like you to take things as quietly as possible.'

Erin interrupted, 'I'm moving into my friends' cottage this weekend, but I've already got my personal belongings there. It's a stone's throw from here.'

Again Gina felt a strange apprehension. The last thing she wanted was Erin on the doorstep of the practice, and yet what did it matter? She herself and Adrian had lost the intimacy of a short while before, and the most she could hope for was to maintain a professional friendship; therefore his association with Erin was no concern of hers.

'Couldn't you remain at the King's Arms——' she began.

'No, I can't stay on. This is their busiest time, and I really do want to get settled.'

'I can understand that, but as I've already said, I want you to rest as much as possible.'

'I appreciate that, and obviously I'll follow your advice.'

'I'll make arrangements for your blood test and do my best to hurry up the path lab report.'

Erin understood. 'Thank you,' she said quietly.

There was nothing more to say, and Gina indicated silently, by a gesture, that the consultation was over.

'When I'm settled will you come and have a drink with me one evening?' Erin looked at her intently.

It was the last thing Gina wanted, but she could not be blatant, and murmured something vague which did not close the door on the possibility, as she saw Erin out.

'You'll let me know when I've to go for the blood test?' Erin spoke in a matter-of-fact voice.

'I'll get on to it immediately.'

'I feel very safe with you,' came the genuine comment.

Why, Gina asked herself, should Erin be so obviously eager to sustain a relationship? Was it to reinforce hers with Adrian? But that didn't quite ring true, since they had clearly kept in touch during the time that had elapsed since the divorce. Nothing added up, and Gina found herself doubly frustrated.

Adrian came out of his room as Gina returned to hers. His attitude was an invitation for her to spare a few minutes, with which she agreed as he stood aside for her to precede him.

'I think,' she said, coming to the point in a business-like fashion, 'we're dealing with an anaemia.'

'Ah!' he exclaimed. 'And I suppose it's a question of what type?'

'Exactly. Obviously I'm arranging for a blood test.'

'I'm not surprised at your findings.' The words slipped out.

Gina said pertinently, 'I thought you'd have a pretty good assessment.'

He did not react to the implication as he completely changed the subject. 'Malcolm tells me you're going to the Royal Shakespeare Theatre on Wednesday.'

Was that, Gina asked herself, his way of reminding her that, while Erin was in his life, Malcolm was in hers?

'On my day off,' she said, meeting his gaze steadily, 'so I shan't interfere with things more than usual.'

'I don't think the word "interfere" comes into it; we've adjusted well so far.'

Gina wanted to provoke him into betraying his feelings, knowing that it was most unlikely he would do so.

They were aware of each other in that moment, and it was obvious to her that Adrian was silently seeking harmony which allowed him to escape into his relationship with Erin while maintaining a friendly partnership with her, Gina. There was irony in the fact that she was facing precisely the situation with him now as she had done during their marriage.

As they left the room together, their arms brushed and their eyes met and held in an intimate gaze before they went their separate ways along the corridor. Gina flushed with annoyance. Adrian was a man who had the ability to make every woman believe she was the only one in his life, and anger built up into an almost bitter resentment.

* * *

Gina faced the visit to the theatre with a keen anticipation. Not only was it her first visit there, despite staying in Stratford-upon-Avon prior to coming to Chipping Campden, but she was both relieved and relaxed to be having her day off and getting away from the atmosphere of Adrian and Erin. She felt that she had been in a spin-drier since seeing Erin at the hotel, and was determined to escape from all thoughts and conjectures connected with them. Malcolm offered a release from problems and his company was always stimulating. The fact that he was in love with her added to the possibilities; and her feelings for him were sufficiently deep to make him a challenge. She had given him her friendship and there was no pretence between them. Despite his frankness there was also a faintly mysterious air on occasion which had manifested itself intriguingly during their association.

On greeting her at her flat where he collected her, he said immediately, 'I like that little cream jacket over the bluey green skirt and the white blouse, with its frilly top——' He laughed. 'I shouldn't make a fashion writer! But I know what I mean.'

'Thank you,' she murmured. 'The skirt is turquoise!'

'Can't expect me to go in for *shades*.'

'That you notice is pleasant in itself,' she said appreciatively.

He looked at her with a lingering tenderness. 'There'll never be a time when I fail to notice everything about you, Gina.' He added, 'And you're relaxed this evening as though you're enjoying the idea of coming out with me.'

'Of course I'm enjoying the idea,' she said immediately. 'It seems absurd that I've never been to the

Shakespeare Theatre. My friend, Maggie Latham, with whom I stayed, wasn't very keen on going. . . She's in Canada now, holidaying with her brother. I miss her. We were at school together in Minehead and have always kept in touch.'

'I like that,' Malcolm commented. 'You lived in Dunster.'

'Yes; a lovely spot, with its old Yarn Market and Luttrell Castle at the top of the hill standing sentinel over the village—picturesque. I don't go there enough, but my parents are very understanding. You'd like them, and they're still lovers after thirty years.'

'That appeals to you?' He spoke softly and on a note of persuasion.

Was he, Gina asked herself subconsciously trying to discover more about her past, since she had only made the bald statement that she was divorced without a third party being involved? The words, 'without a third party being involved', seemed to be a form of dissimulation, since Erin was still in the picture. However, she argued, that fact didn't invalidate the truth that Erin had not figured in the divorce action.

'Very much,' she said honestly. 'I'd always hoped to follow my parents' tradition.'

He looked at her solemnly. 'It's not too late to do so. Happiness very often follows the lessons learned from mistakes.'

She felt a warmth stir her as she said, 'You're a very understanding person.'

'Love brings understanding.'

'Not always, Malcolm. It can sometimes be responsible for the greatest misunderstanding of all.'

'And we,' he quipped, 'are going out for the evening, not to a psychological discussion.'

Gina laughed and adapted her mood to his.

They drove into Stratford, which was designed in an orderly fashion with the three main streets running parallel to the river and three running at right angles. The central streets still bore the same names as when Shakespeare knew them—Bridge Street, Church Street, and so on—and the buildings preserved many links with the past, with the picturesque half-timbered type of construction redolent of Tudor and Jacobean times. Shakespeare's Birthplace, world-famous, dating back to the early sixteenth century, while undergoing inevitable changes remained substantially as it was so far as the timberwork was concerned. The town was in harmony with the Warwickshire countryside and of typically English appearance.

When they arrived at the theatre, Gina said, 'I've always thought it looks stark, possibly because it's modern.'

'Built, or rather opened, in 1932,' said Malcolm.

The attraction of the building was its river frontage, with a series of terraces extending the whole length of the theatre. Having parked the car, Malcolm and Gina wandered along by the Avon, which glistened in the evening light and threw off stars that danced in the July sun. An eager audience, strolling idly about and colourfully dressed, completed the picture that might have been painted and thrown on an imaginary screen.

'We could have had a meal here,' Malcolm said suddenly. 'There's a fully licensed restaurant and refreshment bars overlooking the river.'

'I like the idea of going back to Campden,' Gina assured him.

She took in the details of the theatre as they joined the throng of the crowds when they went in finally to take their seats. The walls were panelled in dark wood, and she noticed a commemorative plaque in the foyer to the Americans who, with other nations overseas, had supported the erection and endowment of the building. A suspended roof made the acoustics particularly good.

The waves of sound from thirteen hundred people surged up at her, for it was a full house. She felt the thrill and anticipation that preceded the performance, and tension, together with all thought of Adrian and Erin, vanished. Then came the moment when the lights dimmed and the curtain went up, bringing an electric silence, and apart from the intervals the audience sat spellbound, held by a story as old as time and as new as today, emphasising that the years did not change human nature and that romantic love might be decried, ridiculed by the elite, yet remained true to life and ever triumphant.

The applause at the end was deafening and sustained, the well-known principal actor and actress receiving a thunderous ovation until the curtain finally came down and remained down.

Malcolm and Gina went spellbound into the darkening night, where the afterglow dipped its colour into the still river and held the mood by its beauty in which there was a magnificence that awakened an ecstasy deep and fulfilling.

'That's been an experience, not just a performance,' Gina said when they reached the seclusion of the car and drove through the quiet streets. Emotion gave her voice solemnity.

'I'm so glad we came together.' Malcolm put out his hand and touched hers.

'So am I.' The thought streaked through her mind that she was glad Erin had moved out of the hotel that morning, so that there was no question of a meeting. Malcolm would get to know her in due time, no doubt, but tonight she didn't want intrusions or explanations.

'We must make a habit of it,' he said deliberately, his hand having returned to the steering-wheel.

She didn't make any protest, instead she said with a certain eagerness, 'I'd like that. I'd like to see some of the modern plays and the actors and actresses we've got to know through television.'

'Then I shall make a point of taking note of what's on. I'm very fond of the theatre, but confess to not being fond of going on my own.'

Gina thought of Adrian. She had heard him make that remark to Anne only the other week.

'I agree with you. . .but then nothing,' she added unguardedly, 'is much fun on one's own.'

'Your admission heartens me,' he said immediately. 'I must take you to Hidcote Manor to explore the grounds. There are so many rare plants and shrubs from all over the world, to say nothing of the series of small gardens specialising in some particular kind of flower.'

'I'd like that,' she said without hesitation.

'And we must go to the top of Ilmington Down where there's a fine view of Campden nestling against the hillside. There's so *much* to see, Gina,' he added intently.

They had supper in the candlelit dining-room of the King's Arms, and talked easily as the evening ended and Malcolm took her the short distance back to the flat, seeing her in with a protective air that drew them together in a sudden intimacy. He moved closer to her, his gaze resting on her lips as he put out his arms and drew her to him in a fierce possessive intensity.

'Marry me,' he whispered in a passionate plea as his kiss allowed no escape, and he felt her respond as though she had no further resistance.

Gina yielded with a sudden freedom, feeling that her emotions were no longer restricted and that the possibility of marriage, with its security and Malcolm's deep and enduring love, gave to the future a permanence that she valued more than she had thought possible. Was this an inescapable bond?

'I love you,' he murmured, holding her with a suffocating closeness.

She surrendered as though suddenly mesmerised by his intensity, the feeling that she needed him uppermost. Was this love? This desire for fulfilment and the security of marriage?

'Gina,' he whispered. 'There could be so much ahead for us. . . I won't rush you; only say that you'll marry me, darling. . .' His voice was low and pleading.

She felt resolution ebbing from her and sensation overwhelming her as she said, 'Yes. . .*yes*,' and felt his arms tightening about her.

She stood there trembling, feeling that she was in some strange world of fantasy. To marry Malcolm; to know the security of his love and the end of loneliness. Of course it was right and sensible. There would be devotion and fidelity, the past forgotten; the moment of passion with Adrian part of yesterday that had no reality.

'I can't believe it,' Malcolm said, drawing her to the sofa and holding her as though he would never let her go.

She looked up at him. 'Neither can I,' she admitted.

'Everyone knows I'm in love with you,' he said with a smile. 'It won't come as a surprise.' He added hastily, 'At least, not from my side.' He looked at her earnestly. 'I've felt that you were beginning to care, and this evening you were different, as I told you.'

'It's been a lovely evening,' she said eagerly. 'Oh, Malcolm, I'll do everything I can to make you happy!'

'Just love me,' he said simply.

She tensed. 'I will,' she promised, and it was like making a vow.

'I haven't over-persuaded you?' he asked fearfully.

Gina insisted to herself that this was not so. Malcolm was everything that any woman could wish for in a man, and, even if she hadn't fallen in love with him at first sight, she had known tonight that he represented something special in her life and, above all, an escape from the uncertainty of emotional conflict.

'No,' she assured him, feeling a strange unfamiliar love swell in her heart and telling herself that this was the deepest level of loving, which would grow with the happiness she could imagine him inspiring. She liked his humour, his understanding and sympathy, his frankness. She would always know where she was with him, and trust was implicit.'I want us to be lovers after thirty years—like my parents. I want children and grandchildren,' she went on, her voice warm and loving.

He put his arms around her, pressed his lips to hers, and said quietly, 'I'll try to make those dreams come true.'

She looked up at him, her eyes bright. 'You will,' she answered confidently.

'I can't wait to tell them at Mill Lodge,' Malcolm said as he released her. 'I don't think they expected you to agree to marry me so soon, so we shall give them a real surprise. Anne will be delighted; so will Hugh.' He added almost as an afterthought, 'Adrian isn't so easy to judge, although he knew immediately what my feelings were for you. There's been an instinctive understanding between us, but I'm sure he'd never hazard any guesses about your feelings.'

Gina felt awkward. The past, so far as Malcolm was concerned, was dead. She had no intention of asking him about any other women who had been in his life; in the same way that he had made it abundantly clear that he didn't want her to explain, or make an issue of, the past and her divorce. That, however, did not automatically solve the problem. Would Adrian now prefer the truth to be known? Might he feel at a disadvantage? Yet wasn't that ridiculous? His interests were solely involved with Erin.

Nevertheless, the following morning Gina rang him on his private line and asked if he could spare her a few minutes because there was a personal matter she wished to discuss. He immediately agreed, and arrived in her room the moment they had both seen their respective patients.

'I've something to tell you that I'd prefer you hear from me rather than as a general announcement,' she began.

His eyes widened and met hers with a direct, enquiring gaze. 'Sounds ominous.' His voice was deep.

'Only it isn't,' she assured him. 'I just want you to know that I'm going to marry Malcolm.'

CHAPTER SIX

THERE was a moment of tense silence following Gina's announcement that she was going to marry Malcolm.

Adrian said almost formally, 'I wish you every happiness.' His dark eyes looked deeply into hers as he added, 'Malcolm is just the right type for you.'

It was not the kind of comment she expected, but a warm sensation of relief surged over her as she thought of Malcolm and the stability of the future. His love for her seemed a protection, and hers for him gave life a new meaning. Tomorrow was a promise instead of a bleak uncertainty.

'I'd like to discuss the general situation with you,' she told Adrian. She explained how she and Malcolm had taken on trust their respective past relationships. The question was: had the engagement invalidated the tacit agreement, and was it fair to remain silent about Adrian's identity? Equally, she could not divulge it without his sanction.

His response was immediate.

'I have no objection whatsoever to Malcolm knowing that I'm your ex-husband, but won't it put him at a disadvantage—make it awkward all round? An ex-husband has little identity; he belongs to the past, with the lovers—or whatever you care to call them.' He held her gaze disarmingly. 'But a name, an identity, actually in the picture, could be a vastly different matter and invite misunderstanding. You and I won't have that—we've gone through the gamut of emotion and are free from its perils, so there's no question of disloyalty.'

Gina felt a sense of relief as she added, 'And we could always be honest and tell the truth should it be necessary. After all, Hugh doesn't know, so it's better this way.' She spoke with confidence, adding, 'Now the book will be closed.'

'Succinctly put!' he said, nodding his agreement. His look was searching. 'I must admit I didn't think Malcolm would win quite so soon, but I'm not surprised you're going to marry him.'

'The cliché that we never know tomorrow being so true.'

Why, Gina asked herself, even then, couldn't he be open with her about Erin? Not that it mattered, but it would have set the record straight. All the frankness had been on her side.

'Will you be marrying soon?' The question came rather abruptly as Adrian darted her an enquiring look.

Gina forced him to hold her gaze as emotion touched her.

'We haven't made any plans—it was only decided last evening. Malcolm's commitments have to be considered, as well as Hugh's and yours. Assistants don't go sailing off on honeymoon in the six months of their trial period.'

His smile was encouraging, his voice low. 'There are always exceptions. . .' He changed the subject abruptly. 'Hugh and Anne will be delighted. They've adjusted remarkably well to Jill's situation, and now that she's home——'

'I'm seeing her any minute now,' Gina volunteered.

'You'll help her to adjust.'

'She's been difficult while in the nursing home.'

Adrian looked serious and then said spontaneously, 'This is where a woman in the practice is invaluable.' He paused before adding, 'I shudder to think of your deciding to leave us and join Malcolm at some future date!'

She gave a little cry of dissent and said impulsively, 'I'm not at all sure I approve of husband and wife working together.' She realised the implication the moment the words were uttered.

'There's a gentle irony in the observation, since you have no aversion to working with an *ex*-husband!'

In that moment his previous words, 'We've gone through the gamut of emotion and are free from its perils, so there's no question of disloyalty,' re-echoed, and could not have been more eloquent.

'You've already summed up our relationship,' she reminded him significantly.

He stiffened slightly. 'And I must get out on my rounds. Thank you for taking me into your confidence. Obviously I shan't know anything about the engagement until it's formally announced.'

She felt that his attitude was in the nature of a dismissal and they parted without further comment.

Anne saw Gina come through the communicating door into the family quarters and steered her into the dining-room, moving and speaking quietly. Her usual buoyancy was missing and she looked worried.

'Jill is wholly unapproachable,' she said appealingly. 'We've tried not to make an issue of all this, and to ignore its implications, but it's as though she wants to start a quarrel and resents any kindness shown to her.

If we'd taken up an arbitrary attitude I honestly believe she would have been more amenable.'

Gina was not surprised. 'I'll have a talk with her,' she said encouragingly. 'This is bound to be a difficult phase.'

Anne sighed. 'It isn't what one would have wished for her.' There was no self-pity or condemnation. 'We want to help but we don't quite know how. Hugh's dealt with it purely on a physical basis, concerned only about her health. Oh, he hasn't fussed, but merely asking how she is achieves the wrong result. . . You've been so good, Gina, and I feel wretched; yet if she'd had the child——'

'Jill is in many ways a child herself,' Gina said gently.

Anne nodded. Gina felt that it was all wrong for the older woman to be sad. The Fawcett household was normally full of happiness and joy. Now it had been cast in shadow, not wholly by events, but by Jill's attitude towards those events.

Gina said with determination, 'Leave Jill to me. I don't want you upset any more than is inevitable. . .in fact I won't *have* you upset,' she added firmly.

Anne put out her hand and clasped Gina's. 'You've been so supportive. I do understand that all this, from Jill's point of view, is very traumatic, but it's almost as though she resents any attempt on our part to help her.'

'Guilt,' Gina said quietly.

'That's the last thing I want to build up. Understanding is the only answer where there's been folly.'

Gina looked solemn as she said quietly, 'You and Hugh are very special people.' With that she went to see Jill in an almost belligerent mood.

Jill was lazing, bored, in a deep armchair in the sitting-room, a book discarded, a half-full cup of coffee on a table beside her.

'Another visit to Exhibit A,' she greeted Gina. 'My pulse doesn't need taking——'

'I'll decide what your medical needs are, Jill,' Gina put in.

'I feel bloody. . .no energy—and my parents are driving me mad!'

Gina squared her shoulders. 'And I don't suppose it occurs to you that you're driving *them* mad? Have you asked yourself what you'd have done without them? You've had their moral support, their physical care, and no recriminations. They've behaved as though your operation were an appendix, leaving you to tell them just what you wished. No condemnation. . . I know, because I've talked to them. I'll make every allowance for your post-operative reactions, but when it comes to your parents—no, Jill. *No!*'

There was a heavy silence before Jill burst out, 'You're right, of course. I've made them the whipping-boy. . . I still can't believe that it's all happened; that, after all I'd *said*, I'd be such a fool. I'm not particularly fond of champagne and I wasn't keen enough to think in terms of getting into bed with anyone to take the pill the moment I got the prescription. I *told* you—the idea of sleeping around was, and is, revolting to me. I'll never forgive myself for being so *stupid*——' She added, 'I'd got my life planned and thought in terms of living with someone before I married, being on the pill, having it all worked *out*——' She stopped, put her hands up to her face and burst into tears.

Gina sat silently. Jill would not, she knew, take

kindly to sympathy; she would appreciate the tears being ignored. When the paroxysm was over, Jill said almost calmly, 'My parents have been marvellous. . . You're right. When I think of my position if they'd been different. . . Oh, Gina, I've made such a mess of things. Will I ever be given another chance?' Her tear-filled eyes pleaded.

'There's always another chance,' Gina assured her. 'With resolution——'

'Resolution! You give me consolation. . . I've been a pretty beastly specimen, and now it seems that I'm whining because I've wrecked everything, and am playing the goody-goody. But I've got to tell someone how I feel, and you've been so good to me; so understanding.' Jill shook her head. 'Everyone has been good, and that includes Malcolm; he didn't make me feel embarrassed.' She paused, aware of Gina's gaze intently upon her and remembering how she had previously admitted that she had a crush on Malcolm, and would go to bed with him if he wanted her. Now, should she tell Gina that she was genuinely in love with him, and the fact that she was only eighteen made no difference to the depth and sincerity of her feelings? Jealousy stabbed her as she thought of Malcolm and Gina because, from the beginning, she had sensed the obvious attraction he had for Gina; an attraction she could not ignore. But she tried to convince herself that if a woman wanted a man and was determined to get him, she would succeed, and that her own youth was no disadvantage. Better not to confide in Gina, who would no doubt dismiss the idea as no more than girlish folly, an extension of the crush. A rebellious mood possessed her as she dwelt on Malcolm's feelings: he had treated her with a gentle sympathy and friendliness. She might have been his sister. But, she told herself fiercely, she would fight no matter how great the odds or competition.

Gina checked up on a few physical details and then said quietly, 'I want your assurance that you won't indulge in any more unpleasant moods and that I can rely on your word about your parents. You can never repay them for their support over this, and the loving way they've dealt with the matter.'

Jill tossed her hair back from her face, her expression solemn. 'I was sincere just now. Why doubt me?'

'Because I don't want to see your mother's happiness undermined further. She and your father deserve——'

Jill cut in, '*I* know what they deserve—my love and consideration. You said there was always another chance.' She sighed deeply. 'I wish I were made differently. I don't understand you "even keel" people—must be very dull!'

'That depends on what you mean by "even keel". Constantly fluctuating moods don't make for harmony in life, and you wouldn't tolerate them in other people.' Gina spoke severely.

'I would in Malcolm,' came the swift retort.

Gina didn't want to discuss Malcolm. It would be different when their engagement was announced. She had no illusions about Jill's reception of the news and was prepared for jealousy.

'I must get back to my other patients,' she exclaimed evasively.

Jill looked suspicious. 'You don't want to discuss Malcolm, do you?'

'That was not the object of my visit,' came the

smooth reply. 'I think we've covered all the ground that's important. Bear in mind all that's been said and you'll be surprised how much better you feel generally.'

Jill was studying Gina intently, but all she said was, 'I won't let you down where my parents are concerned and I'll try to deserve that second chance. Thank you for all you've done.'

To Gina's surprise, when she returned from her rounds at lunchtime Malcolm's car was outside Mill Lodge, and immediately she sought him out in the family quarters where everyone was gathered, including Jill, who was sitting on the sofa. Hugh and Anne looked happy, and it was obvious that she had made her peace with them.

As Gina entered the room Malcolm strode towards her and took her hand, saying, as he addressed everyone, 'I had to come to tell you the news. Last night Gina promised to marry me. I took a chance on getting you all here together.'

Jill gave a little distressed cry, looking at Gina almost accusingly as she burst out, 'You didn't give anything away when you saw me a short while ago!'

'Why, no; we had to tell you together.'

Hugh and Anne expressed their delight, Anne putting her arms around Gina and kissing her warmly. Hugh kissed her cheek and said, 'All the happiness, my dear.'

And at last the attention was focused on Adrian, who looked at Gina intently for a fraction of a second, and only they knew the drama of the event, as he extended his good wishes.

Jill murmured something almost unintelligible before

adding, 'You're not going to rush off and get married quickly.' It was said in a breath.

The fear in her voice was not lost on Malcolm. 'We shall arrange things to suit everyone's convenience,' he replied, looking from Hugh to Adrian.

Adrian almost repeated the sentiments he had earlier expressed to Gina. 'Just so long as you don't lure her away from us professionally.'

'Ah!' Hugh gave a near groan.

Malcolm laughed. 'Let us get married before we plan the future! Gina knows that Alec Delaney is all that I could wish for in a partner.'

'Thank heaven for that!' Hugh said fervently.

Gina beamed. 'You're giving me every encouragement to believe I shall stay the course!' She laughed. 'But a lot can happen between now and our wedding.'

'Prophetically spoken,' Adrian put in swiftly.

Gina met his gaze for a second, and then said quickly, 'I've got a patient to see——'

Anne said, 'I'd hoped you might be able to have some lunch.'

'The supreme optimist, my wife,' Hugh chuckled, 'even after twenty-one years of marriage!'

'It's a miracle that I've managed to see you even for this short while,' Malcolm put in. 'I'm on my way to Cheltenham General, and I'd better get a move on.'

'Suppose you all come to me on Sunday morning for a celebration?' invited Gina, looking around her and allowing her gaze to rest in Adrian's for a split second longer than the others.

It was agreed, and they went their separate ways, Malcolm and Gina walking arm in arm to the front door. He said, 'I'll see you as soon as I can this evening, darling. I've asked Alec to stand in.'

'And I'm not on call. Adrian is.'

'Adrian's a bit of a dark horse where his relationships are concerned. If we could get him married,' Malcolm added with a smile, 'we'd make a good foursome. The three of us get on well together already, don't we?'

Gina tensed as she said, 'Yes,' and changed the subject.

It was after she had seen the lunchtime patient that Gina looked down at her recent mail and was aware of Erin's blood test result from Cheltenham Hospital—'Iron Deficiency Anaemia'—and sighed with relief. Pernicious anaemia would have been grave. She flicked down the intercom and asked Mrs Greyson to make an appointment with Miss Foster as soon as possible. Erin, she realised, was not a person to fuss and her heavy periods, weakness, loss of weight, had been accepted with stoicism, for which Gina commended her.

'What about lunch, Dr Gordon?' asked the secretary.

'I'm not hungry and—oh, Mrs Greyson, I was going to look in and tell you, but I seem to have been moving in a trance. Dr Villiers and I are going to be married.'

There was a delighted gasp at the other end of the line. 'We thought that would happen,' came the sage reply. 'Oh, we *do* wish you every happiness.'

'I'll see you later. . .everyone else knows.'

'It's very exciting. . .and I'm going to bring you some sandwiches and coffee. Can't have you starving before your next patient! There'll just be time.'

'I'd like you all to come and have a drink with me when we can arrange it,' Gina said spontaneously.

'That would be lovely.' Mrs Greyson hesitated, and then said warmly, 'Dr Villiers is such a fine man. Everyone thinks highly of him.'

Gina glowed.

A little later she accepted gratefully the coffee and sandwiches Mrs Greyson brought. 'You're very good to me,' she said.

'Then show your appreciation by eating them all. . .and I'll ring Miss Foster. Mrs Cummings has cancelled her eleven o'clock appointment tomorrow, so we have a gap.' She smiled. 'I'm not giving any secrets away if I say that Mrs Cummings isn't pregnant after all! She was so thrilled, she had to confide in me when she couldn't speak to you!' She hurried to the door, and as she was about to go from the room Adrian appeared and stood aside to let her out.

'Come in,' invited Gina. 'Have you had anything to eat?'

He hesitated.

'Which means you haven't.'

'I had an urgent prescription to give and a long telephone call. . .there's not been time.'

'Splendid,' said Gina. 'We can share these.' She held out the plate towards him, studying him as he took a sandwich and bit swiftly into it. 'Did you want to see me for any special reason?'

'Just to know if you've heard the result of Erin's test.'

She handed him the report and indicated the patients' chair, sitting back in her own at her desk. As he read, she watched him carefully, noticing the obvious relief that accompanied the verdict.

'Thank God it isn't pernicious,' he said. 'A high-calorie, protein, mineral and vitamin diet, together with oral iron and——'

Gina tensed; she felt irritated. 'I do know how to treat the condition,' she said slightly acidly.

There was an awkward silence before he exclaimed, 'I was speaking out of turn.' His voice was clipped. 'My apologies. Erin is your patient.'

Gina felt embarrassed. 'I didn't mean to sound pompous. I too am grateful we can deal with the problem.'

His gaze was faintly puzzled, as though he was trying to assess her mood and failing. He was about to speak, but paused and fell back on silence.

Gina explained, 'I didn't use the right word; it wasn't pompous exactly——'

He cut in with a quiet rebuff, 'You resented my interference.' He held her gaze with faint criticism. 'I was merely thinking aloud, not for one moment assuming that you wouldn't be aware of the right procedure.'

'We seem to have a genius for misunderstanding each other.' There was a half-apologetic note in her voice.

'Which isn't exactly surprising.'

'Meaning that doing so is a legacy from the past?' She spoke quietly. The silence in the room was heavy and full of suspense.

'I think that would be a fair assessment, but there's no reason why we should reminisce, particularly at this juncture.'

She felt rebuffed and her temper rose. 'No reason whatsoever,' she retorted sharply.

They looked at each other stormily for a second, then his attitude changed.

Gina thought of Malcolm and the fact that she would be seeing him this evening. Nothing said between her and Adrian was really important, and it was ridiculous to argue with him. He was a baffling character no matter what the circumstances.

And then suddenly his voice alerted her. 'I've a request to make.'

'Request?' she echoed almost nervously.

'Favour, if you like. Would you have any objection to my bringing Erin with me to your engagement celebration on Sunday?'

Gina stared at Adrian aghast; it was the last thing she expected and her amazement was obvious, but she tried to conceal it as she met his gaze and said swiftly, not wanting to appear either hostile or half-hearted, 'Why, no! By all means bring her; we should be delighted.' She added, trying not to sound pointed, 'Malcolm hasn't met her, has he?'

'No. I want him to.' He added sympathetically, 'She's been too exhausted with the move to meet new people, but now that she's settled and can follow your advice to rest, she can find the strength to go out from time to time. Also, it will be a good way for her to get to know Hugh and Anne.'

Gina reminded herself that she had been irritated by his secrecy over Erin, but now he was being frank she was astonished, and not wholly receptive to Erin being drawn into the circle. But she exclaimed, 'A good idea!'

There was a moment's silence before Adrian asked tentatively, 'There's just one thing: would *you* invite her? She might feel awkward if the invitation was merely passed on by me.'

It was the last thing that Gina wanted, but she agreed, adding, 'I'm hoping to see her at eleven tomorrow morning and can mention it then.'

Adrian looked pleased. 'Thank you, Gina.' As always he gave her name significance. 'It will be a very splendid occasion. I don't think I've ever seen a happier man than Malcolm.'

'We're very lucky,' Gina said.

Slightly confused, Adrian said hastily, 'And, of course, you look happy too.' He gave a smile that transformed his face and added to his attractiveness. 'May the future atone for the past.'

'For you too,' she said genuinely.

An inscrutable look came into his eyes and he murmured, 'My next patient is due. . . I appreciated the sandwich and your co-operation,' he went on almost abruptly, going to the door as he spoke, and there was an element of fantasy in their parting as he hurried away.

Gina flicked down the intercom and Mrs Greyson said that the first patient of the afternoon batch had arrived, volunteering the information, also, that Miss Foster would be able to keep the eleven o'clock appointment tomorrow. To Gina, the situation was somehow unreal, and drama built up from it. Just how significant was this new development, and what were Adrian's feelings?

Gina concentrated wholly on Malcolm as she awaited his arrival that evening. She warmed to the memory of

Mrs Greyson's words, 'Dr Villiers is such a fine man,' knowing them to be true; she hadn't a doubt about him in any direction. He was exactly what he seemed—a man to be trusted, who loved life and believed in working hard and playing hard.

He arrived with a superb arrangement of red roses.

'I thought I'd be different,' he admitted, 'and spare you having to deal with them while I was dying to kiss you!'

'Oh, Malcolm, they're lovely!'

'And,' he said, 'I hope you'll think the same about this.'

She stared down at the engagement ring in its case which he had opened, and gasped at its beauty. An oval sapphire, surrounded with pricked-out diamonds, looked back at her. As he slipped it on her finger a tremor went over her and she clung to him as he kissed her with passionate earnestness, whispering, 'I love you, my darling, now and always.'

She held out her hand and admired the ring. 'It's exquisite,' she murmured. 'I didn't dream I'd have it today.' There was a catch in her voice as she added, 'If I'd chosen it myself it couldn't have been better.'

'Would you have preferred to choose it?' He spoke anxiously.

'Oh, no! I like surprises.'

'And I wanted the bargain sealed,' he said with a smile. 'I bought it in Cheltenham today. Engaged to *me*. I'm the proudest man alive.' A chuckle escaped him. 'You've bewitched me—you know that. From the very first moment, too.'

Gina was touched and there was a lump in her throat. 'I want to make you so *happy*. I've said it before, but it's true.' It suddenly seemed like a debt of honour.

'Being my wife, loving me, will achieve that,' he insisted. 'There's nothing else in life I desire, as I've already said.'

A shadow touched her. Was it wrong not to tell him about Adrian? And yet what purpose would be served? A sensation in the pit of her stomach made her feel slightly sick. She would have to behave as though she had only recently met Erin and would need Erin's co-operation to sustain the deception. In addition, that phase had not been discussed between her and Adrian, since neither had taken the matter into account.

A little later she told Malcolm that Adrian wanted to bring a friend, Erin Foster, to the engagement party. She had just come to Chipping Campden.

Malcolm was delighted. 'That's splendid! I've never heard Adrian's name linked with any woman. As I said, he's a dark horse and, apart from his divorce, he never mentions the past.'

'Miss Foster is my patient,' Gina said evasively.

Malcolm looked at her questiongly. 'Do you like her?'

Gina kept as near the truth as possible, as she replied honestly, 'I don't know her well enough to give any informed opinion. At the moment she's a frail, almost sad person—accounted for, no doubt, by her health.' Gina thought of the past. She had never *known* Erin. She had feared, even suspected, her role in Adrian's life, and this latest development had added to the intrigue. But it was of no consequence now, since her own life was settled and she was going to marry Malcolm.

'Anyway,' Malcolm said easily, 'let's hope they find happiness together. That would round things off very well. Any friend of Adrian's is a friend of mine.' He drew Gina into his arms. 'Only *we* matter at this moment,' he added as he parted her lips in a passionate kiss.

Gina spoke to Adrian the following morning before surgery started. He appreciated her point about the time factor where she and Erin were concerned.

'You have only to mention the situation to her, and you can rely on her discretion. It isn't as though you were ever friends, so very little will be concealed.'

Gina wanted to remind him that she had never been given a chance really to know Erin; she was always a mystery, then as now.

'Reverting to the party,' she said, 'you'll have to leave it to me to judge if she can stand up to it physically. There's a certain excitement, and people can be tiring.' There was a note of authority in her voice.

'Even if she can't come, the invitation will be the most important thing,' Adrian told her.

Gina wondered why.

Erin arrived punctually at eleven and came apprehensively into the room. Gina greeted her at the door, noticing that her brown skin was touched with blusher, but that her wide blue eyes had a hunted expression, which she tried to conceal with a smile.

Gina told her the facts of her illness, quietly and explicitly, finishing with, 'So you see, we can deal with this without any trouble.'

'I wondered if I might need a blood transfusion.' Her voice, much to Gina's surprise, broke.

'You had pernicious anaemia in your mind,' Gina said gently.

'Yes; and the complications and fuss——' She stopped, distressed by all the possibilities. 'I want to get back to work,' she explained, controlling herself.

Gina found it difficult to assess the situation. She had imagined Erin to be a composed character, and now she found that she was very vulnerable. Was this an emotional reaction, or a purely physical resistance to illness?

'We'll soon have you better,' Gina promised. 'But you must give yourself a chance and get the benefit from more rest.'

'I'm so thankful to be settled in my own domain. No matter how good a hotel is, one's home means everything.'

Gina nodded her agreement and then asked, unexpectedly from Erin's point of view, 'How do you cope with people—I mean, do they tire you beyond limits?'

'Some do. I don't know which are the worst—those who talk non-stop, or those who never initiate a conversation. The former make one's head swim; the latter tax one mentally. . . Why do you ask?'

'Because, if you feel up to it, I'd like you to come to my engagement party on Sunday. Dr Villiers and I are going to be married,' Gina told her.

Erin gave a little cry of delight. 'Why, that's wonderful! I've heard nothing but good about Dr Villiers, and I know Adrian thinks very highly of him. I'd love to come to the party.'

Gina looked at her steadily. 'Adrian will be joining us and could bring you,' she said easily. 'There's just one thing—I'd be grateful if you went along with the idea that we've only recently met and that you are, as is true, my patient. Malcolm knows I've been divorced, but not that Adrian is my ex-husband. By the same token, I've not pried into his past. It's wiser this way.'

Erin looked grave, but she said, 'You can rely on my not mentioning the past. I see your point. I never quite know what *is* wise when it comes to confidences.' She added irrelevantly, 'It's wonderful that you're going to be married again.'

Gina noticed that she didn't mention Adrian or suggest that it would be ideal if he could marry again. What *was* her life? And why did she not mention the past, even to her doctor? In her privileged position Gina was free to ask any questions pertaining to the patient's health, for emotion and emotional problems played a major part in that same health. As it was, she felt instinctively that silence was the best policy. It did not escape Gina's notice that Erin was delighted at the news of the engagement, but she could not assess the significance of the fact. It struck her forcibly that Adrian was obviously eager to stimulate his association with Erin, or he would not have wished her to be asked to the celebration. When it came to it they were both unknown factors.

Erin said quickly, 'Are you going to be married soon?'

'We've only just become engaged. Nothing has been settled.'

Gina wanted to ask her why she had come to Chipping Campden, but felt that she would receive only evasion, since the reason must be obvious— Adrian.

'I'm very much looking forward to meeting Dr

Villiers and the Fawcetts,' said Erin. She added, 'I'm taking it for granted that the Fawcetts will be there on Sunday.'

'Oh, yes; they're dears.'

'So I believe.'

Gina found it difficult to accept the fact that she was talking to Erin without undue tension; that she was a patient partly provided the explanation, but, for the rest, her relationship with Adrian invited conjecture which Gina found intriguing. She wrote out the iron prescription and listed the diet, stressing the fact that Erin must not consider working for at least a month.

When it was time to go, Erin said appreciatively, 'Thank you for being so kind to me. I'd like to think that we could be friends and have an understanding, particularly now that I'm your patient.'

Gina received the plea with sympathy and a generosity of manner rather than effusive words. On parting, she added, 'Perhaps you could arrange with Adrian about Sunday. It's a short distance, but too far for you to walk.'

'But I *could* drive, because one drink is all I can take, and that would leave Adrian free.'

'Then I'll see you on Sunday,' Gina said pleasantly. And, as Erin left, she wondered why every time Adrian's name was mentioned Erin gave it significance.

The party was a great success. Malcolm exuded happiness, Hugh and Anne contributed to the sparkling conversation and *joie de vivre*, Adrian and Erin were relaxed and natural; only Jill looked glum as she faced up to Malcolm's engagement. Gina kept close to Malcolm feeling that his love for her illuminated the future and wiped out the fears of the present. Once or twice she met Adrian's gaze, and nostalgia surged as though their marriage were still a reality.

Malcolm whispered to her, '*Darling*,' as he passed from Hugh to Erin, and there was a wealth of love in the endearment.

She looked at him with a caressing smile, warming to his love and feeling revitalised by his presence.

Anne moved closer to her and whispered, 'Do you think Adrian and Miss Foster will soon be following your example? He's very attentive.'

Gina answered brightly, 'I wouldn't like to hazard a guess. I don't know enough about their relationship.'

Later, when it was time for the buffet meal in the dining-room, Gina noticed that Adrian and Erin were missing, and she moved into the curved hallway where she had a view of the sitting-room without being observed.

At the sight of them, she tensed and a strange emotion quickened her heartbeat. Their arms were around each other and Erin's head was on his shoulder.

CHAPTER SEVEN

GINA stepped a few paces into the dining-room. Malcolm hovered and said, 'Darling! You look startled. . .and where are Adrian and Erin?'

They appeared even as he spoke, Adrian's gaze going immediately to Gina's as he took in the familiar pattern of the buffet scene, the moment frozen in memory, she thought, telling herself that this was her engagement party. But as she looked at Adrian standing there, powerful, his dark eyes magnetic, her heart was thudding as she realised with a devastating shock and dismay that she was still in love with him and could hardly bear to remember seeing him with Erin in his arms.

For a second she felt faint with emotion. It wasn't possible. Here she was with Malcolm, wearing his ring, surrounded with good wishes. The juxtaposition was so full of irony. She told herself that she was fantasising; that her reactions were of jealousy engendered by the fact that she now had proof that Adrian and Erin were more than friends. It changed the pattern, deepening, also, the mystery. Why had they not married? She shuddered at the possibility and concentrated on the task of playing hostess, while Malcolm opened the champagne. Panic assailed her. She wanted to be alone to face up to the dark secret which already tormented her. If only she did not care for Malcolm, it would be easier; but she could not withdraw from the bargain at its inception.

Hugh proposed a toast and Adrian seconded it. Malcolm responded heartily, putting his arm around Gina's shoulder as he added, 'May we celebrate for many, many years, not only Gina's and my relationship, but our friendships which are so much part of our lives.'

Gina watched Erin. Were she and Adrian lovers? Had they been all along? She intercepted their glances, which seemed full of understanding.

Jill said bluntly, 'You're miles away, Gina.'

Gina jumped and made some facetious comment, turning to Malcolm and smiling. Jill had only eyes for him and craved his attention, having moments when she hated Gina and longed to cause trouble.

Everyone ate heartily of the delicacies and Hugh stimulated the conversation, so that Gina had the satisfaction that all was going well. But to her it was bizarre. An engagement party at which the ex-husband was a guest and the newly engaged fiancée still in love with him! Was it possible? She tried to avoid looking at him, but every now and then her gaze was drawn to his as though by some mesmeric quality and her pulse quickened alarmingly. He looked poised and calm, talking to Malcolm and laughing spontaneously. Obviously he was not in any state of turmoil, or was he such a good actor that he could play any role? Wasn't that what he had apparently been doing all their married life? The man who really didn't want any permanent commitment.

Anne contributed a great deal to the success of the occasion, raising just the right subjects, enjoying the buffet, intrigued by Adrian and Erin, whose relationship she found difficult to assess, while liking Erin, whose expression in repose was a little sad. She thought Gina was tense, but attributed it to emotion and happiness.

It was after the meal was over and they were drinking their coffee that all eyes turned to Erin, who had lost all her colour, was trembling and drawing her hand across her forehead, as she murmured, 'I'm so sorry, but. . . Adrian, would you take me home? I'm not going to faint, but I feel. . .' Her voice trailed away weakly.

Both Adrian and Gina went over to her.

'You can rest here,' Gina said with encouraging sympathy. 'Lie down on the bed.'

Erin looked agitated. She wanted to be in her own home.

Adrian took command. 'I'll get her home,' he said forcefully.

'So sorry. . .' Erin was pathetically apologetic. 'But I'm all right. If I get back now, I can get to bed. Please don't spoil the party.'

Adrian had arm-lifted her to her feet, and Malcolm immediately lent his support. Gina said gently, 'I'll come to see you a little later on.'

'So sorry,' Erin murmured again, clinging to both Adrian and Malcolm.

Gina noticed how supportive and tender Adrian was, how tightly his arm enfolded her. There was no question of irritability because he was having to leave the party; rather was it the suggestion of a husband taking his wife home as a right. Gina accompanied them to the car and stood with Malcolm, watching as it drove up the High Street.

'Too bad,' said Malcolm. 'But Adrian will look after her.'

'Yes,' Gina echoed, feeling wretched and depressed, 'Adrian will look after her.'

All she could hear was Adrian saying, 'You'll forgive me if I don't return? He looked at Gina with professional authority. 'You'll be coming along soon, won't you?' The suggestion had been that, engagement party or no engagement party, her duty was to her patient.

Hugh, Anne and Jill left soon afterwards; a damper had been put on the proceedings and they felt it was kinder to leave Malcolm and Gina alone.

When they had gone, Malcolm said ruefully, 'A foretaste of things to come—when we're married and both on call! But at least I can kiss you, darling. There were moments just now when I thought engagement parties ought to be for just the two people concerned! You look so beautiful in that blue and white dress. Tantalising with your perfect figure. . . Oh, Gina, I want you so desperately!' As he spoke he drew her into his arms, his lips parting hers in a passionate gesture that made her draw back quickly after the breathless kiss. She knew, even in that second, that she could not go to bed with Malcolm, feeling as she did about Adrian, until after she and Malcolm were married. And while the fact didn't make sense, it was a deep emotional reaction.

'I must go and see Erin,' she said a little later.

'It would have been a good idea to keep her here for a while.' He tried to sound patient.

'No; everyone wants to be in their own home when they don't feel well. They can relax and recover far more quickly.' She added appealingly, 'I blame myself for believing she was up to the excitement.' And even as she spoke, she wondered how much Erin's relationship with Adrian had contributed to her near-fainting episode. Had there been some dramatic event?

'I'll come back this evening,' Malcolm said hopefully. 'We could go out for a run and have a meal at that tucked-away little restaurant, the Thatched Inn, near Ilmington Down.'

Gina agreed. She felt hollow and depressed, finding it difficult to put on a cheerful act and realising that this was the pattern for the future, since she could not renege on her promise to Malcolm, and that it was up to her to build a new life with him. Adrian represented the past; Malcolm was the future.

It was a shock when a little while later Adrian opened the door to her at Erin's flat. 'Erin's in bed,' he said quietly.

Gina had to adjust herself to looking at him, knowing that she was in love with him. He seemed larger than life as he stood there, his dark eyes meeting hers, his mouth set in a firm line, his whole personality overwhelming her with its intensity. He was the man she had married, slept with, loved, hated, doubted, dismissed, and was as much a part of her as an arm or a leg.

'The celebration was far too much for her,' he said emphatically.

'Meaning,' Gina flashed back, 'that I shouldn't have allowed her to come!'

He studied her intently. 'Meaning that you took a too sanguine look at her condition.' He spoke frankly.

There was annoyance in the air.

'One has to consider the attitude of the patient when making a judgement,' she countered. She was aware of him as he stood there, dominant, accusing, and all she wanted was to be in his arms. How desperately she loved him, she thought with despair. How could she marry another man, feeling as she did? Yet how could she let Malcolm down and return to a barren future? She had become accustomed to Malcolm's love, indulgence; to be without it, while longing for Adrian, would be living in a wilderness.

'But the final decision rests with the physician,' he said firmly.

She shot at him, 'There are other factors to consider. I can't judge Erin's emotional life and, normally, that's taken into account. She may have problems of which I'm unaware.'

Adrian said immediately, 'If a patient wishes to discuss those problems, then she or he will.'

'Meanwhile,' Gina flashed, 'the doctor works in the dark.'

They faced each other stormily.

'I suggest you go up to her,' he said, his voice cool.

All that Gina could see in that moment was Erin in his arms.

'Very well,' she agreed sharply.

Erin was distressed and apologetic. Her pallor was marked, her lassitude obvious as she lay back against the pillows.

Gina noticed that she was wearing a lacy jacket in a

soft shade of pink, which gave her an appealing appearance, and her large eyes were wide and helpless as she said, 'I'm so *sorry*. I've spoilt things, but there was nothing I could do about it. The excitement and emotion were just too much. I blame myself—I shouldn't have accepted the invitation.' She added, 'Adrian was adamant that I should get into bed, and I must say I'm grateful to be here.'

Gina took her pulse and blood-pressure, tested her heart and asked, 'Are you under strain of any kind?'

There was a moment of breathless silence after which Erin admitted, 'The stress of moving—the apprehension about getting a new job.'

Never, Gina thought, any mention of emotion, or her life so far as human relationships were concerned.

'You know,' Gina said deliberately, 'the great thing for a doctor is to treat the whole person, and if she's unaware of that person's problems then she's unable to diagnose or really to help.'

'I appreciate that,' came the swift reply, but further confidence was not forthcoming, and it was as though a blind had come down between them. 'I shall be all right tomorrow. I *am* much better generally, but today was too different. . . Have I spoilt it all?' It was a pleading enquiry seeking reassurance. 'To have to work on the day of your engagement party is the last thing. . .you're very kind, Gina.' It was said quietly and with appreciation.

Gina noticed that Erin made no comment about Adrian having his day interrupted. His part in it all seemed accepted as being perfectly normal, even when he came into the bedroom a little later to enquire.

'Well?' His voice was anxious.

'Nothing that rest won't take care of,' Gina said swiftly. 'Rest and freedom from strain,' she added pointedly, looking directly into Adrian's questioning eyes.

She and Adrian left the bedroom a few seconds later and went downstairs into the sitting-room.

'How *is* she?' Adrian spoke anxiously.

'You know the pattern after a near-faint in her condition. Blood-pressure low, pulse slow to begin with and then rapid.' She looked at him with disarming directness. 'You have influence over her, and your word will count more than mine,' she added pointedly.

There was an awkward silence before he exclaimed, 'We've spoilt your day. . . I'm so sorry.'

'We've'. That one word, Gina thought, identified them and had more significance than a dozen. She reminded him, 'There's the evening. . .and we're doctors, not film stars.'

He said quietly, 'Thank you, Gina.'

His voice thrilled her; emotion overwhelmed her. Nothing in her life was valid any more, and she dreaded the hours when she had to face up to the reality of the situation. An eternity seemed to have passed since the announcement of the engagement.

'You will be keeping in touch with her?' She tried to sound professional.

'Yes,' he said as though it were a foregone conclusion.

'I don't think there'll be any drama, but I don't like the idea of her being left alone for too long. Equally, she doesn't want to be disturbed by the doorbell.'

Adrian said naturally and without thinking, 'I have a key.' He added, 'As you know, I'm on call.'

Startled, Gina merely nodded.

During the next few weeks Erin improved sufficiently to contemplate starting work, and Gina faced up to the disturbing fact of Malcolm not knowing the truth about her relationship with Adrian. Already she found herself being evasive on occasions, which distressed her, for her relationship with Malcolm, irrespective of love, was full of understanding and harmony, their pattern for living identical, so there was no question of breaking the engagement. She couldn't live a barren life of solitude and would never find anyone who suited her needs like Malcolm. Adrian was like a spike in her heart, her desire for him not diminishing with time, and his apparently deepening friendship with Erin stimulating her jealousy. His attitude towards her, Gina, did not change, but there were times when he was challenging and ready to argue, the discourse always ending on a note of affability, when it would have been perilously easy to read more into his intense looks than was meant. Did he ever remember her as his wife? Or think of the night they had spent together? Every day she wondered if he would announce his engagement to Erin; the suspense was agonising. He spent a great deal of his time with her, and Gina always heard the echo of his words: 'I have a key'! That could be accounted for when Erin was first ill, but he had made it sound the most natural thing in the world. Did he expect to be regarded as Erin's lover? Wasn't there a certain defiance in his attitude?

The question of Erin joining Malcolm and his partner

arose when she was ready to start work. He still had only a temporary secretary, and Adrian's reference was all Erin needed to secure the post.

'I can give her the highest praise,' Adrian said one evening when he, Erin, Malcolm and Gina were together in Erin's cottage, she having invited them to repay hospitality received, and the question of the post arose.

'And that,' Gina said pointedly, 'is something you can rely on, Malcolm.' She drew back quickly: she was not supposed to be *au fait* with Adrian's past associates. 'I'm sure that if it weren't for Mrs Greyson being the proverbial "treasure", you wouldn't have the opportunity of Erin's services.'

Malcolm said quietly, 'I'll take your word, and second both yours and Adrian's with my own. The job awaits you, Erin.'

Erin gave a little murmur of delight. 'I couldn't be happier!' She looked around the sitting-room with its oak beams and chintzy furnishings. 'Now I really feel I'm settled.'

Gina noticed how at home Adrian appeared, pouring out the drinks and giving Gina just the right sherry, as though he had briefed Erin on what brands to order. He was relaxed and obviously pleased about her joining Malcolm. Several times she found her eyes meeting his, and immediately lowered her gaze. It was impossible to avoid the familiarity their relationship imposed and she felt that Malcolm must notice the intimacy of the communication.

It was the following evening, when the August sun was setting and throwing a crimson glow on the ancient houses in the High Street, that Malcolm took Gina in his arms and parted her lips in a passionate kiss, his desire like a flame between them as the sexual side of their relationship took precedence.

She felt his hand on her breast and drew back, almost naïve in her resistance. She could not face up to the reality of Malcolm as a lover; only marriage seemed to justify her sleeping with him in the circumstances. There was no logic in it, she knew, but logic and emotion seldom if ever met.

Malcolm moved away, his manner solemn. 'I don't want to pressurise you, but the fact that you've been married——' He broke off, tacitly implying that he was not, after all, threatening her virginity.

In that moment the secret of Adrian's identity seemed to represent disloyalty. Guilt touched her and she decided to get Adrian's sanction for the truth to be told.

'I'd like a new life to begin when we're married,' she said, unconsciously pleading for his understanding, 'or do you think that's fanciful? Particularly these days.'

'I can only respect your wishes,' he replied, 'but you can't blame me for wanting you, darling. I did so from the first moment I saw you. It wasn't all pure romance,' he admitted honestly. 'There was a terrific physical attraction.' His voice was low and he looked at her searchingly. 'But you shall have your wish for a new life. When it comes to it, I like to think you're a romantic at heart.' And with that he kissed her tenderly as though sealing a pact.

The following morning Gina rang Adrian and arranged to see him at lunchtime. She had no doubt but that he would fall in with her wishes, which meant she could tell Malcolm the truth that evening.

Meanwhile Malcolm called at Mill Lodge to have a quick word with Gina, as was his custom whenever possible, but Jill hailed him and drew him into the sitting-room. She had a predatory expression as she said with satisfaction, 'They're all out. . . Coffee?' She was thrilled to have him to herself and wanted to prolong the meeting as she added pointedly, 'You must have a minute or you wouldn't be here.'

'I'd like a coffee.' He was conscious of Jill's grey-green eyes, dark with desire, and fully aware of her reactions to him, which always put him on his guard. She had a challenging air and looked extremely attractive in a scarlet skirt and white blouse; her chestnut hair shone in the sunlight and fell loosely about her elfin face.

Martha, the Fawcetts' daily 'treasure', made the coffee, and after the door closed behind her they talked a trifle stiltedly before Jill said significantly, 'Do you know anything about Gina's ex-husband?'

Malcolm stiffened. He had no intention of discussing Gina. 'The subject is not a matter for conversation,' he said sharply and warningly.

Jill was immediately bold and defiant; a little secretive smile played about her full red lips. 'Because it's such a mystery. She never mentions him, or refers to the past.'

'That has nothing whatever to do with you,' he insisted.

'But *you* don't know his identity.' Her words had an element of attack; her gaze held his with a certain defiance.

He put his cup down impatiently, feeling resentment at the intrusion. His mouth hardened as he said harshly, 'That's our business.' The words rushed out, despite himself. The past suddenly had dramatic significance and, for the first time, his ignorance mocked him.

'In which I have an interest, since I overheard a somewhat frank discussion which told me who the mystery man was.' Jill looked pleased with herself.

'A question of putting two and two together and making five, no doubt.'

'On the contrary, it was very simple,' she persisted coolly. '*Adrian* is Gina's ex-husband. It so happens that I don't like to see you fooled.'

The sudden silence was as heavy as that which preceded thunder. Malcolm looked both shocked and disbelieving as he found himself echoing Adrian's name with incredulity, adding, 'I don't believe you!' Amazement mingled with accusation. Malcolm's face had paled, his eyes darkened with suspicion as he rapped out, 'This is sheer fabrication! It doesn't enhance my opinion of you.'

Jill's voice sharpened on the edge of jealousy and emotion. She had never dreamed she could want anyone so desperately as she wanted Malcolm, or be so jealous of the women he loved. Her stomach churned as she rapped out, 'You have a simple way of proving me wrong. Ask them if it's true, and why the secrecy.'

'Don't introduce a sinister note,' he countered. 'You don't deceive me, Jill, and I suspect your motives.'

She reddened and clasped her hands so tightly that the knuckles showed white. She hadn't intended to introduce an arbitrary note, or to betray her feelings so palpably.

'My motives are bound up in your interest. No matter what the position between you and Gina regarding the past, you certainly didn't dream that Adrian was involved,' she challenged him. 'Although I'm not in the least surprised. There's always been just that *something* in their manner towards each other.'

'Nonsense; you have a vivid imagination.'

She said sagely, 'Only people who've once been intimate can simulate a casualness that's quite so perfect.' Her eyes hardened. 'They've fooled my parents.'

Malcolm got to his feet. 'I don't want to hear any more,' he told her sternly, his gaze meeting hers with a criticism that made her cringe.

She cried urgently, 'I don't like your being deceived, made a fool of—I——'

His expression silenced her. He was both angry and accusing as he strode to the door.

'Listen, Malcolm,' she pleaded.

'Goodbye, Jill.' With that he was gone.

Gina was not able to see Adrian that lunchtime. He was called to a premature birth and snatched a moment to speak to her on his way out of the house. He had reached the front door when he added, 'By the way, obviously you know that Malcolm's invited me for a drink with you both this evening?'

'I knew he was going to.' Malcolm had mentioned it when he had rung her after he had seen Jill. The idea of a threesome dismayed her, and she was a little puzzled by Malcolm's spur-of-the-moment tactics which left her no room for manoeuvre. Also she was disappointed that her talk with Adrian had to be postponed, finally consoling herself that another day would not materially alter the situation. She knew that Adrian had a tight schedule and that this present case would not allow any time for personal discussion.

Gina arrived at Malcolm's flat, which was situated in the cigar-shaped middle part of the High Street, in a mood of expectancy, tinged with nervousness. An evening *à trois* with Malcolm and Adrian would inevitably be in the nature of an ordeal, and when she saw Malcolm a sudden apprehension touched her. His expression lacked its usual enthusiasm and was almost solemn; his mouth—invariably curved into the semblance of a smile on the slightest provocation—was set into a hard line.

She asked instinctively, 'Are you all right?'

Malcolm had nerved himself for the ordeal, convinced that Jill's story was false. He could not be natural, and said swiftly, 'Perfectly. . . Adrian's here.' He inclined his head towards the sitting-room and avoided any demonstration as he let Gina precede him.

The atmosphere was tense when Adrian got to his feet as Gina entered. Without realising it, her eyes were fearful and sought his instinctively, mutely asking if something was wrong. Adrian looked baffled and murmured a few words about its having been a hectic day.

Malcolm had already given Adrian his whisky and he poured out Gina's dry sherry, set it down somewhat deliberately on the side-table by her chair, took his own glass and moved to the chimneypiece, where he stood looking forbidding, the silence overpowering as he paused before saying, 'You'll have sensed that this is no ordinary meeting.'

Gina's eyes darkened, the pupils dilating, her lips parting and remaining half open in a questioning gesture before she asked, 'What's wrong?'

Malcolm stiffened, his heart thudding. Adrian looked faintly alarmed as they waited for Malcolm to speak, and when he did so his voice seemed to ring through the room accusingly as he said, 'I'll come to the point. I just want to know if you are ex-husband and wife.' He looked straight at Gina. 'Were you and Adrian once married to each other?'

Gina gasped. Presented to her like that, it seemed the ultimate disloyalty. She paled slightly before saying, 'Yes.'

Malcolm looked from her to Adrian, his gaze accusing. So he had criticised Jill unjustly, and he was not prepared for the reaction that set his nerves tingling. *Adrian and Gina.*

'Why,' he demanded, 'the secrecy?'

Adrian's voice was firm, his attitude belligerent. 'There was no question of secrecy; rather it was a matter of discretion.' He took his stand as though protecting Gina from any contumely.

'You see,' Gina explained hastily, 'we hadn't told Hugh, or anbody, and we thought it might be awkward. And when you and I agreed to let the past. . .well, we knew we could always tell you if necessary, and it would have had to come out when we were married——' The more she talked the worse it seemed; an innocent decision became somehow an act of treachery.

She winced as Adrian said coolly, 'It isn't an easy matter to explain how amicable a divorce can be, allowing the two people concerned to be completely free of each other.'

There was a second of silence. Malcolm could not analyse his feelings. Being faced with the reality didn't, when it came to it, seem so traumatic as hearing the truth from Jill.

'It sounds facile to say it now,' Gina murmured, 'but I was going to talk to Adrian only today so that I could tell you the truth this evening. I made up my mind,' she said, looking with wide honest eyes at Malcolm, 'to tell you; but I couldn't do that before Adrian knew of my intention. This was agreed when we decided to remain silent about our relationship. My coming here and meeting Adrian was quite fortuitous.'

There was a note of solemnity in Adrian's voice as he said, 'I give you my word that our marriage in no way detracts from your engagement. It's past and belongs to yesterday.'

Malcolm's expression was changing; the hardness was giving way to a generous, understanding gentleness as he looked at Gina, having been through the gamut of emotion during the past twenty-four hours and seeing his future wrecked once Adrian came into the picture.

Gina was trembling and, although it was a warm evening, she was cold. Her fondness for Malcolm, the fact that he was, she freely confessed, a panacea for the pain of her love for Adrian, made the prospect of losing him from her life a shattering blow. Without him her future would be bleak; with him came the hope of being a true wife and partner, which would in time make her feelings for Adrian unimportant. Adrian had Erin and it would all work out, she told herself.

'I shall have to get used to the truth,' Malcolm said, relaxing with every second that passed, gaining strength from Adrian's completely frank assessment. He stood there self-assured, confident.

Gina put in, 'I'm so terribly sorry I was prevented from telling you myself, Malcolm. Please believe me that I hadn't recognised that keeping it secret was wrong.'

Malcolm moved to her side, picked up her hand and kissed it. 'I believe you,' he said. 'I believe you both. It was just a shock.'

'How did you find out?' Adrian asked suddenly.

Malcolm hesitated and then replied, 'I don't think that matters.' He did not want to cause any breach in the relationship with the Fawcetts. He would have a word with Jill and stress his displeasure, even though what she had said was right.

Gina cried almost instinctively, '*Jill!*'

'I'm afraid I didn't give her any quarter,' Malcolm said, not resorting to further pretence.

Gina was under no misapprehension. If Jill could make trouble, she would have no compunction about doing so. Her feelings for Malcolm were obsessional.

Adrian said with authority, 'We'll tell everyone, so there can be no possible misunderstanding. That applies to the staff as well.' He looked at Gina, expecting her agreement and getting it immediately. It would be a relief for the past to be known and the pretence over. Adrian had put it succinctly when he had said, 'I give you my word that our marriage in no way detracts from your engagement. It's past and belongs to yesterday.' Yet, as he stood there, Gina was acutely conscious that he had been her husband and that it was now almost a matter of honour for her to obliterate the fact and give all her loyalty to Malcolm. Thoughts were treacherous and she must banish them whenever they touched emotion.

Adrian's attitude made it simple: he was completely detached and had handled this scene with a sincerity and sang-froid that were not a contradiction. What was he thinking as he sat there, one leg crossed loosely over the other, seemingly relaxed, his expression inscrutable? And, while his eyes met hers, they told her nothing. She looked away and concentrated on Malcolm, who had the appearance of a man who had come through a storm into the peace of calm waters. It was his nature, she thought, to face up to any problem, solve it, and put it behind him. He would not, she knew, drag the past up, or seek to know its secrets. He had taken their word, and it was enough.

Adrian said discreetly, 'I have a patient to see, so if you'll excuse me. . .' He got to his feet as he spoke, and Malcolm made no protest, grateful for the prospect of having Gina to himself.

It was a strange moment in Gina's life as Adrian looked at her and said, 'Goodbye, Gina.' It held a finality like that which came when closing a book at the last page. . .

CHAPTER EIGHT

GINA faced Adrian the following morning as they met as usual before surgery, feeling strained, almost apprehensive. The previous evening had an almost dreamlike quality about it, and her emotions were still taut, her thoughts unruly. Malcolm's attitude had not changed after Adrian left and he had confessed that, while shocked by the revelation, he was relieved to be put in the picture, particularly after the previous evening when she had made it quite plain that she was not prepared to have a sexual relationship before marriage. That decision threw the past into relief.

Adrian began without preliminaries, 'We must tell Hugh—let them all know.'

His manner had changed in some subtle fashion, leaving him withdrawn, his voice holding a note of politeness that excluded any suggestion of emotion. He looked at her with a steady inscrutability and it was impossible to know what he was thinking. A wall seemed to have come between them. As she sat down in the patients' chair while he seated himself at his desk, she noticed his grey suit and light blue shirt, which emphasised his smooth tan. Her gaze rested on his lips, which were firm but, on occasion, curved into gentleness and humour. In no circumstances did he lose his air of masterfulness.

'Malcolm should be with us.' It was a tentative statement.

He frowned and, like an actor throwing away a line, replied, 'That's up to you.' His scrutiny was unnerving. He added generously, 'Malcolm is such a fine man that he'll never make it an issue.'

Gina appreciated the praise which she knew to be genuine. 'Then I'd like him to be there.' Her heart slowed down a little, a rising temper died. If only Adrian were not such a challenge and she could look at him with indifference instead of an acute sexual consciousness which robbed her of all power to think rationally. She had no illusions that, from now on she would be under the microscope, for Malcolm would not be human if he could discount her former relationship with Adrian. She was touched by Adrian's praise of Malcolm and she envied him his nonchalance over the matter. The thought rushed through her mind that Jill would be disappointed because her dramatic announcement had not produced any disastrous changes on which, no doubt, she had counted.

'Then that's settled. I shall be glad when everyone knows the truth,' Adrian said.

'So shall I.' She sighed, then, 'Our judgement in the beginning seemed valid.'

'But after your engagement it was a tacit disloyalty without any intention of deception on our part.'

'I regret that I didn't tell him. Jill only won by a day.'

Adrian drew her gaze to his for the first time in a disturbing detachment. 'It's of no consequence now.'

Faint colour rose in Gina's cheeks. He might have been bored with the issue.

'None,' she agreed. 'And I'll tell the staff—spare you the irritating task.'

There was no mistaking his relief as he said, 'Thank you. I'd be grateful.'

Everything he said, Gina thought, was normal, but the manner in which he said it removed the last shred of intimacy, and she knew that their previous camaraderie had vanished. Sitting in his patients' chair, feeling the sun on her hair, inwardly she wept as though her heart had received a blow and was hurting, as it thumped heavily in her breast.

He added crisply, 'We don't want any drama.'

'I have no intention of creating it.' Her words were precise.

He pursed his lips and frowned. 'I'd like to know how Jill found out.' There was anger in his voice.

'Probably overheard us talking on some occasion——' Gina stopped, confusion in her large lustrous eyes.

'Or sensed it. Secrecy about the past can invite suspicion and conjecture. Jill, in any case, is very sharp and doesn't miss a trick.'

How true that was, Gina thought, sad in her disillusionment about Jill, who could so easily have come to her, if only to confirm her own conclusions. It was highly unlikely that she'd had irrefutable proof.

Adrian went on, 'She should have been a better judge of Malcolm's character than to imagine he'd be affected by any tales she could tell. I'm very glad that young lady will have been taught a lesson. . . I'll have a word with Hugh and find out if we can see them this evening.'

As he spoke, he got through to Irene Greyson and found that Hugh was in his consulting-room, a patient due any minute. Adrian dialled his private number, heard his pleasant, 'Mr Fawcett,' and asked if he, Gina and Malcolm could see him and Anne that evening, receiving the cheery affirmative with the reservation that, as Adrian knew, he was on call. Hugh insisted on taking his turn, while Adrian equally insisted that, unless it was vital, Hugh was spared all weekend working.

'About six-thirty,' said Adrian. And it was arranged.

Gina got to her feet. There was an emptiness in her stomach and her mouth was dry. It was like the curtain of a play coming down. This was the end of the drama, with the main characters going their separate ways from now on, their secret shared by those around them.

'You can speak to Malcolm,' Adrian said, already on his feet and moving to Gina's side as she turned towards the door. 'If he isn't free he'll understand if we have to see Hugh on our own.'

Gina nodded and exclaimed, 'Erin can juggle his appointments!'

Adrian suggested with fervour, 'Secretaries are worth their weight in gold.'

Gina added, 'I'm sure Erin is that.'

Adrian's expression softened. 'I'm sure too.'

With that he opened the door and Gina left him.

Hugh and Anne received the news with amazement. Jill's expression was as dark as her startled eyes.

'I must admit,' Anne said in her honest fashion, 'that I'd wondered who the Mr X was, particularly as he was never mentioned.' Looking at Adrian and Gina in turn and taking into account the harmony that had always seemed to exist between them, she wondered why they hadn't made a success of their marriage. Another man or woman? Obviously nothing permanent.

Gina looked apologetic. 'It wasn't a matter of deception so much as the wrong idea of discretion. Doing the wrong thing for the best of reasons.' She looked at Jill with a steady, unnerving expression.

Jill's manner was challengingly insolent. She deliberately gazed at Adrian and then Malcolm.

'A bizarre situation. . .make a good play,' she remarked.

Hugh frowned; he did not like his daughter in her present mood and was at a loss to understand it. He said fervently, 'I'm glad we're now in the picture; it strengthens the bond. I always say that if people want you to know anything about their lives, they'll tell you; so why ask questions?'

'You're far too trusting, Daddy.'

Jill's words went home to Gina. It *was* like a play, the drama increased by her own feelings for Adrian, and while she avoided meeting his gaze she was conscious of his subdued manner and that, having made the announcement, he became withdrawn and silent as if to suggest that he had no intention of enlarging on the issue. He refrained from giving Jill importance by commenting on her remark.

Malcolm broke the sudden awkward silence by saying in a voice ringing with confident happiness, 'Gina and I are being married at Christmas.'

The words shattered the unreality and brought Gina face to face with fact. Did Adrian remember their wedding-day on April the fifteenth at the little church at Dunster? She felt his gaze upon her, but when she raised her eyes to meet his he seemed to look through her. And in that moment all that Gina could see was Erin in his arms.

'Christmas!' Jill echoed the word involuntarily. It seemed so soon.

Malcolm had pressed for that date and Gina had not opposed him, grateful for the understanding he had shown in his acceptance of the situation between Adrian and herself. It endeared him to her, his attitude deepening the love she felt for him and making her realise anew how fortunate she was to have such a man with whom to build a future. She squared her shoulders and took a deep breath, telling herself that time and circumstances would kill her love for Adrian. At the moment it was heightened by his relationship with Erin and the suspense thus created.

'Splendid!' said Hugh heartily. 'Although we shall miss you when you're on your honeymoon.' He was going to say to Adrian, 'Shan't we?' but pulled himself up. Introducing that note of intimacy would be wrong. The fact brought home the implications of the present impasse and that it would take a little while to make the necessary adjustments. He glanced at Anne and knew that their thoughts met. Jill's exclamation and attitude had not been lost on him either, and he felt uneasy. He wondered if, had he known the truth about Adrian's and Gina's relationship, he would have accepted her in the practice. Now he wished fervently that the revelation would not destroy any of the previous harmony. Looking at Malcolm, he was aware of his relaxed manner and the ease with which he accepted the facts, thus contributing to the present friendliness and removing any strain.

'We're going to tell the staff, Hugh,' Gina said a few

seconds later, adding, 'Unless, of course, you'd prefer otherwise?'

Hugh replied immediately, 'On the contrary, I think you're wise. We shall all know where we are then.'

'And that the truth can't be leaked from any other source.' Malcolm said pointedly, looking straight at Jill, who was trembling with jealousy and chagrin because her scheming had brought only Malcolm's disapproval.

Gina looked at Hugh with obvious gratitude. 'Thank you for believing that we had no intention of deceiving you.'

Hugh made a little grunting sound. 'I'm sure that's the last thing. You had a point, and we must see to it that nothing changes as a result of the knowledge.' He glanced from Gina to Adrian. 'Anne and I value your friendship, as we do Malcolm's too.'

Anne murmured her warm assent, and Malcolm reciprocated.

The gathering broke up. Hugh had a late consultation with a colleague, Malcolm said he was taking Gina out to dinner and Adrian was seeing Erin.

It had been a heavy surgery, with the aftermath of holiday ailments mostly due to excess sun, food and drink, so that several patients had come home to recuperate, vowing in future to stick to the countries they knew, rather than venture to those where hygiene was an unknown quantity and conditions were generally primitive. Gina had written out the right prescriptions, given the right advice, and felt exceedingly weary as the door closed and the session was over. It had been a very hot day without any breeze, after a spell of cold rainy weather.

Mrs Greyson came in at that moment. 'Just a few letters to sign,' she said brightly.

Gina thought how calmly she, Avril Lane and Janet Westbury had reacted to her news about her marriage to Adrian. After the first exclamations of astonishment, they had accepted it as though it were an everyday occurrence.

Adrian came into Gina's room while Mrs Greyson was there. He too had finished.

'Hot and sticky,' he said, by way of greeting.

Irene took the letters which Gina had signed, and moved to the door. 'My room is nice and cool,' she said with a smile of farewell, as she went out.

'They've accepted our relationship without any difficulty,' Adrian commented. 'I must say I feel far more relaxed. There was always a slight tension before, when one couldn't talk of the past. Even though we may not have realised it.'

Gina both loved and hated seeing him on their own. Loved his presence and yet hated to know that the world stood between them.

'You're obviously with Malcolm this evening,' he added briefly.

'Yes—we're having something cold at my flat.' She paused. Would he tell her what he was doing?

'I'm at home too,' he said. 'Erin will look in.' His voice was matter-of-fact.

Gina nodded, her heart quickening its beat. 'She's really better, and very happy with Malcolm, isn't she?'

He smiled, a smile of satisfaction. 'It was just the job she needed.'

What, Gina asked herself with suppressed fury, were his true feelings? Why couldn't he be frank? And why hadn't she the courage to ask him if they were lovers? His solicitude for Erin was always uppermost, his expression changing when her name was mentioned. And even as she allowed her thoughts rein, Gina knew that she must discipline herself and keep personal matters out of her calculations so that she could view Adrian with detachment. Only then could she hope to lessen his importance and thus be completely loyal to Malcolm. She didn't know what he had come into her room for at that moment. His manner had remained withdrawn since the truth about their relationship had been known a week or so ago.

She looked at him coolly, telling herself it was time she followed his lead. 'What can I do for you?' she asked formally. At least she could avoid further discussion about Erin.

He jerked his head up, surprise in his eyes as he took the hint. 'I'd like you to see a problem case for me,' he replied. 'As I've said before, you're good with emotional issues, and a woman's angle is invaluable.'

'Praise indeed!' There was a trace of cynicism in her voice as she tried to adopt an impassive professional attitude.

He gave her a quizzical look. 'I don't think I've ever failed to appreciate your excellent psychology.'

'Solving other people's problems is so much simpler than one's own.'

'Even in your own life my statement is valid. You've tackled divorce and imminent remarriage admirably.'

It was not what she expected him to say, and it unbalanced her. Did the comment invite her to allude to his own position? She suggested, 'Because you haven't followed my example it doesn't mean that you——'

He cut in, 'My reactions don't come into it.' His voice was steely. Was he, Gina asked herself, protecting Erin because she had been his mistress all this time?

She hardened her expression, her eyes cold as they met his. 'I'll do my best,' she said, her voice crisp. 'May I ask briefly what the problem is?'

'A Mrs Merton, who's on the point of leaving her husband to go to East Africa with her lover.'

'Oh!' She sounded rather surprised. 'Nothing out of the ordinary.'

'No.' It was his turn to be cynical. 'Except that the husband wants her and refuses to agree to a divorce.'

Gina sighed as she said, 'It's usually the woman who refuses to grant a divorce.'

'True.'

'But she can get a divorce on her own application after she and her husband have been apart for five years.'

'That sounds as though you're on her side already.'

Gina shook her head. 'Not necessarily. But I don't like a dog in the manger and I don't call it love.'

'That's what Mrs Merton says.' There was a touch of irony in Adrian's words. He had stood by Gina's desk as he talked, looking down at her in the manner of one who did not intend to stay. Now his gaze held hers and he said, 'You'll give the case a fair assessment. The patient has lost a stone in weight and her nerves are raw.'

'And in the last analysis only she can make the decision, unfortunately,' Gina said sadly.

'Talking to you may give her a new angle, enable her to know her own mind that much better.'

Gina raised her gaze to meet his for a brief second. 'I'll do what I can.'

'*Love!*' Adrian suddenly snapped, voice raised.

'Thrones are lost for it; men and women murder for it; the ignorant laugh at it.' Gina added, 'And we have patients who are ill because of it.' Her eyes had a burning intensity in their lustrous depths.

All Adrian said was, 'You and Malcolm are very lucky to have found each other and to be free to marry. . . Now I must go. I'll leave Mrs Merton to you. She'll fit in with your appointments, of course.'

With that he left.

Gina remained sitting at her desk in what seemed an empty room. And the words she heard echo were, 'You and Malcolm are very lucky to have found each other and to be free to marry.' Again she came back to the question: Was Erin married? She dismissed the thought and concentrated on clearing her desk. When she left the house, the practice quarters were empty, and she congratulated herself that she would have time to shower and change before Malcolm arrived.

When, later, she greeted him, he said, 'You look, and smell, beautiful.' His kiss was passionate and she clung to him, wanting to reciprocate and think only that in a few months they would be married. His attitude had not changed, and he spoke naturally about Adrian without giving his name any undue significance, but as they were sitting with their respective drinks before supper, he asked suddenly, 'Do you think that Adrian and Erin will marry?'

To his amazement, instead of answering him she jumped to her feet and cried desperately, 'Oh, dear God—I've forgotten to visit Mrs Mortimer! She rang Mrs Greyson about teatime and asked me to call. . . Malcolm, I must go to her.' She shook her head in dismay. 'I've *never* left out a patient in my life!' There was alarm in her voice as she hurried to the door, Malcolm beside her. 'She only lives near the church— you do understand?'

'Of course. . . Don't worry; so many of our calls are a wild-goose chase.'

'But this patient is pregnant. . .how *could* I have forgotten her until now?'

Malcolm swiftly opened the car door for her. 'I'd like to think it was love,' he said with an endearing grin.

She raced away, heart thumping and a nameless fear touching her. She had mentally pigeon-holed the visit on her way home, as there had been nothing to indicate urgency. She grew hot with the knowledge that her attention had centred entirely on her own problems.

When she reached the Mortimers' house, she saw, to her dismay, that Adrian's car was parked outside.

CHAPTER NINE

DONALD MORTIMER, the patient's husband, answered the door. He looked faintly annoyed as he said, 'My wife tried to get you at Mill Lodge.'

Gina apologised, 'I'm so sorry to be late. . . I must give Mrs Mortimer my home telephone number,' she added as she stepped into the hall, which was large and furnished like a study. 'Dr Marland——'

'He came immediately after I spoke to him.'

'Is Mrs Mortimer——' Gina's mouth was dry. She had never had this experience before, and it made her feel guilty and ill at ease, hating the fact that she could not very well tell the truth.

At that moment Adrian came down the stairs and, seeing Gina, said deliberately, 'I expect you were held up on a case, Dr Gordon. . . Your patient is in danger of a threatened abortion.' He looked at Donald Mortimer. 'With bed-rest we may be able to avert it. At this stage it's the only treatment.'

Gina looked at Adrian. 'Thank you for taking over.' She was aware of the rather cold criticism in his eyes as they met hers.

Donald Mortimer exclaimed, 'My wife was sure you'd come, but I was worried.'

Adrian moved to the front door, giving the husband a few reassuring words and then saying to Gina, 'Your patient will be glad to see you.' And with that he left the house.

Gina went up to the bedroom, with which she was familiar, having visited Felicity Mortimer on several occasions both before, and during, her almost three months' pregnancy. Now she lay in the large bed, looking attractive in a pink lacy nightdress and jacket which matched the pink and white colour scheme of the room, with its brocade-draped dressing-table and padded headboard of the bed in the same material.

The patient was petite, with chestnut hair and a natural tanned complexion. Her voice was warm as she said, 'It's lovely to see you, Dr Gordon. . . Donald wouldn't listen to me when I insisted that you'd call. Dr Marland suggested that, in view of my spotting, I should have made your visit seem urgent when I spoke to Mrs Greyson.'

Gina agreed and would have liked to have said, 'If only you *had*!'

'I shan't lose the baby—shall I?'

'We hope not; but it means your staying in bed until we're satisfied about your condition.'

'I haven't any pain, and it was only a very little loss.' The words begged for reassurance.

'Then with bed-rest the prognosis is good.'

The smooth brows puckered. 'But if I do have pain and further loss——' her large eyes were solemn and anxious '—would it mean hospital, or a nursing home?'

'Yes,' Gina said honestly.

'And a miscarriage.' She looked rather like a forlorn child as she spoke.

'But we won't think along those lines. Rest can work wonders.'

'I'm very lucky to have living-in help. My dear Lily can do anything and makes work seem a pleasure.

She's a wonderful cook too, so Donald wouldn't be neglected.'

It struck Gina that, while Felicity Mortimer had many advantages, she was not in the least spoilt, and did a great deal for charity and the aged. Her husband was a successful chartered accountant and their marriage was ideal. A child would complete the picture of a genuinely happy couple.

Gina did a routine check. Although Adrian had done it immediately before, she wanted it for her own reference. The blood-pressure and pulse were normal, so was her temperature. She was in fact a very healthy woman, and Gina felt heartened as she prepared to leave.

'I'll come in about eleven tomorrow morning,' she said as she handed Felicity Mortimer a card on which was her home telephone number. 'Meanwhile, if there's any change, you're to ring me immediately—it doesn't matter if it's the middle of the night.'

'You're very good to me,' came the appreciative reply. 'I just pray I'll be all right. I feel fine. Donald panicked this evening. . . Dr Marland was very kind.' She smiled. 'A very attractive man, but it would be difficult to know what he was feeling,' she added irrelevantly.

Gina heard the echo of those words when she saw Adrian in his room the following morning, only on this occasion he looked slightly forbidding as he began, 'Do you often visit your patients as late as your call on Mrs Mortimer?'

Gina was sensitive to the implied criticism and her nerves were taut as she answered, 'Not unless it's unavoidable.' She tried to keep her voice steady.

His gaze was inescapable. 'And was last evening such an occasion?'

Gina felt suddenly that she was on trial, and resentment built up out of her own guilt. 'No. I have to admit I forgot to visit Mrs Mortimer on my way home, and remembered her with shock when Malcolm and I were having a drink. It's never happened before and I'm sure it never will again.' She didn't remove her gaze from his.

The sudden silence was heavy.

'It could have been serious.' There was a note of warning in the words.

Her expression changed; emotion challenged control. 'You don't have to tell me that, and I'm aware that you can't afford to overlook anything in pregnancy.'

He leaned forward and placed his arms on the blotting-pad on his desk, clasping his hands as he exclaimed, 'There's no reason for you to adopt that attitude.' It was said admonishingly. 'We're none of us infallible.'

Gina countered, hardly realising what she was saying, 'You give the impression that *you're* infallible, nevertheless.'

He looked astounded. 'You've no justification for that accusation.'

'You can be very patronising!'

'And you can be unreasonable. Patronising!' he echoed, outraged.

Colour rose in Gina's cheeks as she burst out, 'If it had been Erin who'd made a mistake, you'd have consoled her!' She knew the words were fatal the moment she had uttered them.

A fierce dark anger made his eyes steely as he exclaimed with the sharpness of a pistol shot, 'Erin? Whatever has she to do with this?' He added challengingly, 'Why bring her name into it?' He got to his feet in indignation and as though he had lost all patience.

Gina was almost in a state of shock, her heart racing, her mouth dry. She had behaved badly and plunged further into folly as she answered, 'Probably because you're so full of understanding when it involves anything to do with her.' She added the last damaging words, 'It was always the same!'

The silence that fell was electric; hostility flared as he rapped out, 'Do we have to bring up the past?'

Love, jealousy, self-criticism were all interwoven as Gina struck the last blow. '*Is* it the past?'

He drew her gaze to his and stared her out. 'I think you've said enough.' His tone had an icy dismissal in it. 'May I suggest that in future you do not allow your feelings for Malcolm to blind you to your professional responsibilities.'

How adroitly, she thought, he had avoided taking the subject of Erin any further, and she dared not pursue it, facing the fact that she had handled the scene disastrously and in a manner foreign to her. She got to her feet, which seemed leaden; there was a sickness in her stomach and she could not recall a time when she had felt more wretched. To have given way to jealousy and anger must, of necessity, scar their relationship, which was the last thing in the world she wanted.

Adrian didn't move or speak as she went from the room.

*   *   *

It was two days later, on arrival at Gina's flat at about seven, that Malcolm regarded her anxiously and said, 'Darling, is anything wrong?'

Gina had never been more depressed in her life than since the scene with Adrian. The knowledge that she had brought Erin's name into it seared her. Losing control was not a characteristic of hers, and to have demeaned herself to Adrian, of all people, left what amounted to a strange desolation. His attitude towards her was no more than polite in those moments when their meeting was essential, his eyes cold, his expression calculating. And while she had accepted his somewhat withdrawn manner recently, this was entirely different and gave her no room to manoeuvre. He didn't deviate from practice issues, or use two words where one would do; the easy familiarity which they had once enjoyed had gone.

'Anything wrong?' she echoed, playing for time. 'Why do you ask?'

'Because you were depressed yesterday and it's the same today. There's a shadow in your eyes; and your voice is flat as though talking was an effort.'

She forced a laugh that sounded hollow even to herself. 'You do keep me under your microscope!' she chided. 'We've got a few dicey cases, and it isn't easy always to be objective.'

'This isn't just worry,' he insisted. 'Have I done anything to upset you?'

She burst out, 'Good heavens, no! And seeing you're so sensitive to my moods, I've been annoyed by my forgetting the Mortimer case. The fact that Adrian stepped in doesn't absolve me from responsibility.'

'Oh, *darling*!' The endearment was full of under-standing. He sat beside her on the sofa and took her hand in his consolingly as he added, 'It could have been serious, I'll admit, but no one is infallible.'

'That,' she exclaimed, 'is what Adrian said.'

There was, she thought, irony in the fact. Yet she had accused Adrian of being patronising, deliberately provoking a quarrel for no better reason than that she wanted his sympathy and support. If only she could lose that empty sick sensation in what seemed a hollow body when she went back over it all.

For the first time she sensed that Malcolm reacted to Adrian's name. He released her hand as he com-mented, 'He could have taken you to task. I'd almost forgotten your professional relationship while there's been so much else to consider.

Did that betray unease? Gina asked herself and, in that instant, sat in his chair. Because he had been so understanding in accepting the situation without ques-tion, it didn't cut out the possibility of hurt creeping in, and she said in a rush of love and consideration, 'I told you that my coming to Mill Lodge was quite fortuitous. I'd no idea that Adrian was in the picture since he was on holiday when I first saw Hugh; and it was all very rushed, because he was most anxious for me to start——'

Malcolm cut in, sounding relieved as he said swiftly, 'I'm glad there was no deliberate attempt to get in touch with him again.'

She said fervently, 'Absolutely none. I was amazed when the partner turned out to be Adrian.'

'But you didn't want to back out when you knew you'd be working with him.'

Gina spoke easily, switching back to her feelings at the time, 'No. We'd parted amicably, without bitterness, and the position I was being offered was ideal.'

'I understand.' He relaxed. 'I haven't wanted to pry, or make an issue out of nothing.'

'I'd rather you knew. It isn't very fair to you otherwise—I've just realised that.'

'May I ask if Erin was a factor? Adrian gave us to believe that he'd known her in the past.'

There was a second of silence before Gina said, keeping her voice steady, 'That's a question to which I don't know the answer.'

Malcolm looked surprised.

'It's true.' Gina felt a little of the tension draining away as she added, 'That friendship, or relationship, is a mystery and always has been. She didn't figure in the divorce.' She paused and longed to believe her own words as she added, 'It's of no consequence. Whether they'll marry or not, only time will tell.' She met Malcolm's loving gaze. 'You spoke of their marrying, I recall.'

Malcolm nodded. 'They seem devoted.' It was a fact that filled him with relief. Adrian was the type of man, he argued, who presented a threat; but in that assessment there was no implied criticism, merely an acknowledgement that he was an extremely attractive man who was popular not only with women, but with his own sex.

Gina said solemnly, 'If you would prefer that I left Mill Lodge, I'd understand and be prepared to go. But I wouldn't like to give up my work.' Her heart was sinking as she spoke.

'Darling, I wouldn't dream of asking you to, and,

since everything at Mill Lodge is so harmonious and we understand each other, I see no reason to alter the pattern. Your talking as you've done just now has helped.' He looked at her tenderly. 'Bless you, Gina.' He kissed her forehead. 'So often in life the things we don't understand we suspect. A few words can usually avoid all that.'

'You're the most wonderful man,' she said with deep sincerity.

He smiled. 'Keep talking!' he exclaimed whimsically. 'I like it; and now I want to see your eyes sparkle. How *is* the patient who's responsible for all this self-recrimination?'

'I don't think she'll lose the baby,' she replied, infusing a note of cheerfulness into her voice and knowing that to be fair to Malcolm she must overcome her depression. If she looked at the general situation objectively, the very best thing that could happen would be for Adrian to marry Erin. Her body heated as she recalled her own question to Adrian; '*Is* it the past?' and his reaction that amounted to dismissal. The memory seared her.

She was grateful that Malcolm changed the subject by saying, 'We've got to decide about a house. My flat over the surgery isn't large enough.'

'This flat is mine, as you know,' Gina said tentatively, wondering what his reaction to living there would be. She looked at him questioningly. 'We could make it a base. . .' The words were uttered hesitatingly and with the suggestion that the idea might not be acceptable.

'Until we find a house we like.' He smiled broadly.

'One of the thatched cottages in Ebrington, for preference,' he added.

'That would be a miracle,' she reminded him, thinking how ideal it would be—just two miles away, set on
the hillside, the midday sun casting deep shadows on
its chimneys and thatched roofs. She yearned, then, for
a settled life, the emotional turmoil over and in its
place a happy marriage, with children. Malcolm would
be, she thought, an ideal father.

'We have time,' he said, his voice light and hopeful.

Gina's depression lifted. She was carried along by
his enthusiasm. She had no right, she argued, to cast
any shadows on their relationship on account of
Adrian: it was up to her to concentrate on the future
and be grateful for the happiness it promised.

'It will be fun,' she said brightly, 'sorting out our
respective furniture. I've a few pieces that have been
in the family for a very long while that I'd like to keep,
and I expect you have too.'

He agreed, his attitude co-operative.

She said suddenly, 'We must go to Dunster to see
my parents. It's ridiculous that you haven't yet met
them, but what with the holiday season and their
having been to Madeira——' She shook her head. 'I
don't know where the time goes. . . I haven't met your
parents either; but then they're in Florida.'

'They're coming for a holiday next spring, as you
know,' Malcolm reminded her, 'and you've been wonderful in the way you've written to them even in this
short while.' He laughed as he added, 'Heaven knows
when you'll meet my brother. He's way up in the north
of Scotland. A loner, is Andrew. . .just so long as he

has his wife and the two children. You can't prise him away from his farm.'

'Then we shall have to go to him,' she said cheerfully. 'I feel I know him in some curious way. A straight-from-the-shoulder man.'

'Oh, very much so. Takes after my father, but in looks he's like my mother.' His expression softened. 'Mother's a romantic. She perfectly understands my feelings for you and the suddenness of it all.' He paused before asking tentatively, 'Were you close to Adrian's parents?'

'I never met them; they were both killed in a car crash before we were married. And Adrian's an only child too. His father was a doctor,' she added.

'Ah,' Malcolm's voice was low, 'that part rings a bell. I recall Adrian mentioning that in passing, but our conversations have mostly been in generalities. I see now why that was inevitable.' He spoke naturally and went on easily to another subject, admitting to himself that he was grateful Gina hadn't any in-laws with whom to keep in touch, as no doubt she would have done since it was an amicable divorce.

Gina said a little later, 'It's worked well—your having Erin——' She met Malcolm's gaze levelly.

'Oh, yes; she's already made herself indispensable.' He paused before adding, 'She strikes me as being a very lonely person, and I seldom hear her mention anyone except Adrian.'

'The Mystery of Erin Foster,' Gina said reflectively.

Malcolm nodded. 'I have a feeling that her eventual marriage to Adrian is somehow inevitable,' he said thoughtfully.

'I think you're right,' she agreed, and lifted her head in a gesture of acceptance.

'And we'll begin to look for the right house,' he said. 'I'll get in touch with an agent tomorrow, although what that has to do with Adrian and Erin marrying, I can't think!'

'Association of ideas,' said Gina, a little flame of happiness touching her. 'There's always something exciting about buying a house, although I must say I hadn't anticipated moving from here for a very long while. . . I hadn't counted on meeting you!'

Malcolm put his arms around her and looked down into her eyes. 'Nor I you,' he said as he lowered his lips to hers.

Mrs Greyson said to Gina on her arrival at Mill Lodge the following morning, 'I've squeezed Miss Foster in at twelve-thirty. She telephoned, and I knew you'd want to see her.'

Gina raised her brows and looked apprehensive.

'I don't think there's anything very wrong,' Mrs Greyson volunteered. 'She sounded quite cheerful.'

Gina gave a little laugh. 'We need patients to keep us going, and yet we're delighted when they're well!'

'Job satisfaction,' came the sage reply. 'You've got Mrs Wynn this morning.' It was a warning.

'I think I shall get Dr Marland to go over her. Is he very busy? As if I didn't know!' Gina laughed.

'You could have a word with him now—he's in his room. A pretty heavy day.'

Adrian was at his desk and looked up in surprise when he saw Gina a few minutes later.

'Good morning,' he said smoothly.

She returned the greeting and told him hastily, 'I won't keep you a minute.' She took a few steps into the room, leaving the door ajar.

They looked at each other warily.

'I have five minutes' grace. . . What can I do for you?' he asked.

'See a Mrs Wynn for me. A problem patient who seems to have every complaint in the medical dictionary, with all the tests negative.'

Adrian was immediately co-operative. 'I know. It's easy to overlook the obvious. I'd be happy to see her.' And although his expression was inscrutable, his manner was helpful. They seemed safe while on professional ground.

'Thank you.' She didn't want to think beyond the case in hand and hurried on, 'Mrs Wynn is thirty-two, attractive, makes even casual clothes shriek *haute couture*. No children, and what seems to be an adoring husband.'

The word 'husband' fell on the silence with significance.

Adrian nodded, said, 'Um-m,' adding, 'Is she your first patient?'

'Yes, due now.'

'Like mine. I could slide her in next. Give me a ring when you're ready. My first case won't take long, and you'll have learned the reason for Mrs Wynn's visit by then. It isn't a follow-up?'

'No; I thought she'd run out of complaints.'

'A great virtue, optimism!' His gaze made her heart race. It held a strange disturbing look as though he was asking a question to which there was no answer. A dark shadow seemed to pass over his face as his expression hardened, and it was as though he was rerunning the last scene that had taken place between them.

Gina heard the echo of her words, 'It was always the same,' followed by his challenge, 'Do we have to bring up the past?' Had she really countered with, '*Is* it the past?' The atmosphere changed and a sword seemed to glint between them, dangerously flashing a warning that, even on professional ground, they could not now sustain harmony.

The intercom went.

Gina moved to the door, wishing she had not drawn him into the Wynn case and not deceiving herself as to her motive. She had wanted to see if, by consulting him, she could heal the breach. Colour stole into her cheeks.

'Ring me,' he said briefly as he flicked the switch and told Mrs Greyson to send his patient in.

Gina raised her head a little higher as she went to her room and turned her thoughts to Malcolm, and the peace they knew. Who could tolerate Adrian's changing moods, or hazard any guess as to what his feelings were? And did it matter? Defiance touched her. A few minutes later Joan Wynn came into the room and all personal matters were shelved.

Joan Wynn was the type of woman who could make a sack look elegant; she had a flair for colour and style, and this morning was wearing a cream trouser-suit, with a crimson scarf at the neck. She was slim and beautifully proportioned; her feet were small and encased in soft kid shoes, also scarlet. She had no affectations, but her expression was anxious. Her hair was straight, but expertly cut to curve in on her cheeks, and her eyes were a very dark grey with long lashes that gave her an added beauty. She wore very little make-up and on this occasion had omitted any blusher, so that she looked pale and interesting. Normally her cheeks had a slight flush which suited her and gave depth to her eyes. The omission did not escape Gina's notice and she smiled inwardly.

Without any preamble Mrs Wynn said in a clear, beautifully modulated voice, 'I've got a lump in my breast.'

Despite herself, Gina started. The patient might have said that she had two heads, so great was the surprise. How often had she examined those perfect breasts to make certain that all was well?'

But she said lightly, 'I doubt it, Mrs Wynn. . . Last time I had a look at you——'

'That was three weeks ago.' Her gaze was steady and inflexible.

Gina said firmly, 'I want you to see my colleague, Dr Marland. I think it will be a good thing to have a fresh look at your case.'

The idea appealed. Joan Wynn had noticed Adrian and thought him very attractive.

'I'll do whatever you say,' she said. 'Do you mean now?'

'Yes. I've arranged to ring him.'

'I'd like you to look at my breast first.' She had a pathetic air. 'I've had so *much*. . .and we were to go to Paris this weekend. Last time we were going away I had my ulcer——' She stared Gina out, because all tests had proved negative.

Gina examined her. There was no sign of a lump.

'But I felt it; it was hard—near the nipple.'

'It isn't there now. Your breasts are perfect in every way, but we'll get Dr Marland to go over you and set your mind at rest, although I can't be more positive than I am.'

Joan Wynn looked slightly embarrassed. 'It isn't that I haven't faith in you, Dr Gordon. You've been so patient with me.'

Gina made it easy for her. 'A second opinion is never wasted.'

'I want you to be there. . . Stay with me.'

'Very well.' Gina rang through to Adrian and received the all-clear. 'We can go along to Dr Marland now,' she said confidently, and took Joan Wynn to Adrian's room, making the necessary introduction and subsconsciously watching Adrian's reactions, knowing that he was assessing the patient's type and character, and aware of her obvious charm. He was quite agreeable to Gina's remaining during the consultation, and Avril Lane was summoned to take the patient into the adjoining examining-room and prepare her.

Gina, her voice cool and professional, told Adrian about the proposed trip to Paris and how the pattern was ever-recurring, since, not wanting to go, Joan Wynn retreated into imaginary ill health.

'And you couldn't find any evidence of malignancy?'

'She's absolutely clear.'

'I respect your judgement,' he said firmly and without emotion.

A few minutes later he began his examination with the utmost precision, exploring the lymph glands, making the patient raise her arms, then put her hands on her hips. The silence in the room was tense as Joan Wynn said half appealing, yet with a touch of defiance,

'The lump was *there*!' She raised her hand and selected a spot by her right nipple.

Adrian looked her straight in the face, his eyes challenging. 'Then it has miraculously gone, Mrs Wynn.'

She looked confused and smoothed her hand over her breast. 'I—I don't understand it.' She lowered her gaze and said shamefacedly, 'I must have been over-anxious.' She added, almost forlornly, 'I'm wasting your time, Dr Marland, and yours, Dr Gordon.'

Gina had stood back from the couch and watched Adrian's expert examination, the sureness of his touch, the gentleness and complete concentration.

'On the contrary, I wish everyone were as fortunate as you.' With that he proceeded to examine her heart, chest and lungs, finally casting his stethoscope aside with the words, 'You're in extremely good health. I congratulate you. . .you don't smoke, or drink—I mean, to excess—and your diet is good.'

She looked at him wide-eyed. 'How can you tell that?'

'By the texture of your skin and its suppleness.'

'Then if I'm so well, why do I feel so ill?' came the speedy, rather annoyed, question.

Adrian didn't mince matters; his voice was firm as he said unhesitatingly, 'Because you concentrate on health, Mrs Wynn, and think yourself into——'

She cut in, 'Are you suggesting that I'm a hypochondriac?' Her armour had been pierced. She had not counted on such a rapid diagnosis. The complaint had seemed dramatic and she had relied on Gina taking it seriously. But she had not reckoned on being spoken to so plainly, and coming from Adrian it annoyed her far more than if Gina had upbraided her.

Adrian would like to have answered, 'No; but you're a hysteric—a patient who develops symptoms of illness, mental, physical, or both, for subconscious reasons, in order to escape from anxious or threatening situations. The lump in the breast would be an excuse for not going to Paris.'

Instead he said gently, 'I'm suggesting nothing that isn't for your own good. I understand from Dr Gordon——' he looked at Gina and back to the patient '—that you're going to Paris.' His voice was encouraging as he added, 'That will be just what the doctor ordered—to get away from all thoughts of ailments and enjoy yourself.'

'You can't enjoy yourself if you don't feel well. . .flying doesn't agree with me. I once had a bumpy flight. It was a dreadful experience——'

'Were you sick?'

Colour dyed her cheeks. 'No; but I felt terrible. If I can just go along quietly. . .' she murmured, and sighed, looking quite tragic. 'This—this scare has made me feel all churned up; you don't understand, if I may say so, Dr Marland.'

'I can only give you my opinion. I recommend that you go on holiday and take advantage of the change of scene. I'm sure your husband needs a holiday, as we all do.'

She said meaningly, 'And what are *you* doing about a holiday?' The suggestion was that he should take his own medicine.

'I had mine early this year. . . And now, if you'll excuse me, I have another patient to see,' Adrian said politely. 'Perhaps Dr Gordon can persuade you to take my advice.'

'I'll do my best,' Gina said deliberately, and allowed herself to meet Adrian's gaze for a second. 'Thank you, Dr Marland.' She moved to the door and opened it.

Joan Wynn said, her voice cool, 'Thank you for fitting me in.' She hesitated, seemed about to speak and then hurried to the open door where Gina awaited her.

Alone with Gina, who had warned her that she could only spare a matter of minutes, Joan Wynn said, 'Dr Marland is very direct. Oh, an attractive man, I grant you, but he doesn't know the first thing about me.'

'I agree with him, Mrs Wynn.' Gina didn't waste words. 'Can't I persuade you to go on that holiday? When you first came here today, you made it sound as though the possibility that it would have to be cancelled would be a great disappointment. Yet now you can go with an easy mind.'

'I've had a bad shock,' came the swift retort. 'I like being in my own home when I feel like this.' She got to her feet. 'I'm glad your colleague thinks I'm so healthy. . . I dread to think what he'd be like if I were really *ill*! I feel bad enough as it *is*. But I mustn't keep you.' She got up out of her chair. 'I'd be happy to crawl into bed where no one could bother me. . .' She gave a little annoyed toss of her head. 'Dr Marland saying about my husband needing a holiday. . . Nothing to do with him. Impertinent!' She shook Gina's hand, her grip tightening. 'I don't know what I should do without you,' she said woefully. 'You've helped me through so *much*. I couldn't have kept going without you.'

'Then won't you do something for me?' Gina spoke forcefully.

The dark eyes opened wider and fearfully. 'Of course.' She drew in her breath and waited, tensed.

'Go for that holiday. Once you're away——'

'No!' came the adamant reply, and again, 'No. *I* know how I feel and if I'm well enough. The very thought of it nauseates me.'

Gina knew she was defeated and gave up, seeing her go with a sense of relief.

It was about twenty-five minutes past twelve when Adrian came into Gina's room.

'Mrs Wynn won't go to Paris,' Gina said. 'I'm relieved you've examined her. There's such a thing as being too close to a case to judge it rightly.'

Adrian didn't hesitate. 'This one is a typical hysteria,' he said emphatically. 'A psychiatrist would prefer me to call it a disorder in which the patient develops symptoms of illness, mental or physical, or both, for subconscious reasons. It's a matter of escaping from any situation that threatens plans or preferences.'

Gina knew that it was the correct diagnosis, which she had been reluctant to accept. 'I'm glad to have your opinion. One gets almost confused.'

'Small wonder, when hysteria can take any form, even to the loss of function in some part of the body.'

Gina nodded. 'Once she couldn't use her left hand.'

'Typical!' he exclaimed. 'The symptoms are often quite dramatic, but totally reversible. Recovery is just as sudden as the onset of the disability.' He paused half apologetically. 'But you know all that.'

'This is my first encounter with it. I must admit I've felt out of my depth, because there would appear to be no cause for stress.'

Adrian looked solemn. 'If it continues, we'd better get her to a psychiatrist who'd most probably put her on to psychotherapy tranquillisers. Pity; she's an attractive woman.'

'With a perfect figure,' Gina said unguardedly.

But all that Adrian said was, 'A statue has a perfect figure and is as cold——' He stopped. 'Perfection doesn't attract me.' He seemed far away as he spoke and then added, as though one thought stimulated another, 'You're seeing Erin any minute now, I understand.'

The name fell like silent thunder.

CHAPTER TEN

ERIN only wanted a prescription.

'I thought it would be a good way to see you for a few minutes and tell you how well I feel,' she explained. 'You've helped me so much.'

Gina studied her with professional scrutiny. Her eyes were bright, her brown skin glowing. She had never looked more attractive.

'I'm glad,' Gina said warmly. 'For a patient to be well is the best compliment we can have. You're certainly a good advertisement!'

A little mysterious expression spread over Erin's face, which seemed fringed with happiness. 'Thank you,' she said, and smiled.

Gina thought how strange it was that when Erin's name was brought up between her and Adrian, it always held significance. Yet as she sat facing her, there was no animosity. Faint colour mounted Gina's cheeks as she faced up to the power of jealousy; jealousy engendered by secrecy. She was at a loss to understand why she could accept the likelihood of Adrian's and Erin's being married, and yet shrink from the possibility of their being lovers.

And it was in that moment of silence that there was an explosion as though a bomb had gone off. The sound of tearing metal and the shattering of glass brought them both to their feet.

'An accident!' exclaimed Gina and hurried towards the front door, Erin following. Adrian joined them.

In the street immediately in front of the house, one car had ploughed into another, the debris scattered over the road and partly on the pavement. A man was slumped over the steering-wheel, blood oozing from a head wound caused by a blow from the shattered windscreen. Another man swayed drunkenly from a mass of tangled metal, dazed, as he cried, 'I hit him. . . I hit him! Oh, my God! He's not dead. . .dead?'

Already people had gathered as though appearing from invisible holes in the road, to crowd around the wreckage until Adrian, on a note of authority, took over. 'Stand back! We're doctors—give us room. . . Ah, Officer——' as two policemen drew up and got out of a police car, having heard the crash while on patrol '—if you can keep a clear way and get us an ambulance for this patient——'

He indicated the man at the wheel, who had now lifted his head, his body sliding back in the driving seat as he murmured, 'Some. . .madman hit. . .me——' His face was a mask of grey and red as the blood stained his cheeks.

And suddenly Erin's voice rang out, 'Paul. . . *Paul*!'

Gina heard the startled cry, without pausing in her effort with Adrian to try to assess any other damage, thankful that the injured man reacted to Erin's voice, calling out her name and managing to add, 'I'm. . .all. . .right.' His voice was full of courage, but his head was obviously throbbing and his body must have felt mangled from the jarring.

One police officer was dealing with the offender, who was breathalysed and found to be well over the limit. Shock had made him appear sober and his expression was stark and full of fear. He had little strength in his legs, and propped himself up against the wreckage of his car, which was a BMW.

To Gina, the activities of the next few minutes were like isolated film shots taken at random against an unreal background: Erin explaining that Paul Emerson was a friend of her and Adrian; Paul Emerson recognising Adrian and crying out, 'Adrian! No hospital. . . I'm all right. . .coming to see you. I'm staying. . .at the Cotswold House.'

They got him into Adrian's consulting-room, supported on the examining couch, while Adrian applied a dressing to his head wound. The police, helpful and in command, were relieved that Adrian gave his permission for Paul Emerson to be breathalysed, the result negative, which meant that they had a clear-cut case of dangerous driving against the man about to be taken to the police station.

Gina, who had assisted Adrian and wiped the bloodstains from Paul Emerson's face, studied him other than as a patient for the first time, realising that he was a good-looking man, even swathed in bandages, with dark brown eyes and a firm clean-cut jaw. His lips were bruised and swollen, which gave his speech a muffled intonation as he explained, 'I'd just pulled up outside and taken my seatbelt off. . . My *car*?' He puckered his brows and looked at Erin, who had sat silently in the patients' chair, watching the proceedings with Adrian's permission.

Erin said reassuringly, 'Our garage people will see to it.'

At that juncture the ambulance men arrived.

No one took any notice of Paul's protestations, but Erin got to her feet.

'I'll follow you in my car—it's outside—and if they give you the all-clear I can drive you back,' she said firmly.

'It's only my head,' came the insistent voice. He looked at Erin. 'Thank you,' he said. There was a dazed expression on his face as he allowed the ambulance men to help him into a wheelchair.

'Cheltenham General?' Erin made a statement rather than asked a question.

'Casualty,' came the reply.

'I'll have a word with them,' said Adrian, his hand on Paul's shoulder.

Gina noticed the look Adrian gave to Erin before she hurried ahead. It was impossible to judge its significance. Did Paul Emerson know the truth about Adrian and Erin's relationship? And why hadn't his name ever been mentioned?

Adrian and Gina followed the little procession and saw the ambulance drive away, followed by Erin's car.

'He isn't concussed,' Gina said with conviction.

'Just shocked. He'll hurt like hell as all the bruises come out. I'll get on to the garage and have them take care of his car. It's pretty buckled—a new Vauxhall too.'

'The culprit's BMW rightly got the worst of it.'

Adrian agreed.

'Erin was very concerned, despite her calm exterior.' Gina spoke with directness and watched a certain wariness flash into his eyes.

'We've known Paul for a good while,' he said evasively.

'We've'. The plural seemed to have a life of its own and confuse the issue further. Gina wanted to remind Adrian that he had never mentioned Paul, but knew that might lead to dissension since it was no concern of hers.

Slight confusion spread over Adrian's features, almost as though he were reading Gina's thoughts, and he added hastily, 'This has taken care of our lunch break. I've got a patient who'll be waiting.'

Gina nodded, then asked, 'Ought we to tell Malcolm that Erin won't be back this afternoon? Heaven knows how long she'll have to wait around.'

Adrian answered swiftly and confidently, 'She had the day off.'

'Oh!' How familiar he was with every phase of Erin's life! 'Do you think they'll keep him in?'

Adrian didn't hesitate. 'No; they'll X-ray his skull, but I don't think the scalp lacerations were serious and he was, as you said, not concussed, just shaken; but——' He paused, sighed, and added, 'Cursory examinations are not satisfactory in cases like this.' He walked to the door, and with his hand on the knob his expression told her that he was expecting her to precede him, which she did, hurriedly, and with just a nod as she went into the hall. Outside the house the crowd had dispersed, with only a few onlookers studying the damaged cars, and deciding among themselves that *someone* must have been hurt. The fact seemed to satisfy their curiosity.

Hugh came in from a visit and asked, faintly alarmed, 'What's been happening here?'

Gina explained, and when Hugh realised that the

victim was a friend of Adrian and Erin, said immediately, 'If there's anything Anne and I can do. . . I don't like the idea of Mr Emerson going to a hotel. Suggest to Erin that he comes here where we can keep an eye on him.' He finished, 'See what Adrian thinks. . . I've got to dash. I leave the arrangements to you.' With that he hurried through to his consulting-room.

Gina relayed his message to Adrian at the first opportunity.

'Any news?' She looked concerned. Two hours had passed, during which time they had seen one patient after another.

'No.' He sighed. 'Casualty's always hectic.'

Gina nodded, and told him of Hugh's invitation.

For a second he seemed impressed, then, as though having given the matter due thought, he said, 'On reflection I've an idea that Paul would prefer to be a free agent. It's damned good of Hugh to think of it, and of course I'll mention it to Erin.'

The telephone rang on his private line, and he picked up the receiver quickly.

'Erin!' he said in anticipation, concern spreading over his features. 'Letting him out? Oh, good. How is he? Yes, of course. See you later.' He replaced the receiver and looked at Gina. 'You heard all that. They're allowing him home.'

'In the care of a responsible relative,' Gina said as though reading the hospital notes.

Adrian frowned, but then he asked tentatively, 'Could you possibly hold the fort this evening?' He explained, 'I'd like to keep an eye on Paul.' His concern was obvious. He did not bring Erin's name into it.

Gina kept her voice very steady and efficient. 'I'll be on call.'

'Thank you. I hope you weren't doing anything special.'

She shook her head as she replied, 'We'd only talked of going to Cheltenham to the cinema, but that's of no consequence.'

There was an awkward pause. Gina broke it by reminding him, 'You will have a word with Hugh?'

'Most certainly. I'll give them time to get back to the hotel and finalise the arrangements.'

Gina asked herself where Paul Emerson fitted into the picture and why Adrian was so involved. It was impossible to hazard a guess, for Adrian's attitude gave nothing away. Their eyes met, but they might have been sightless.

When Gina told Malcolm what had happened, he said, 'The man's probably a relative.'

'Erin would surely have said,' Gina suggested.

'Oh, I don't know. . .in the case of an accident, no one follows a normal pattern of behaviour.'

'I suppose not.' She took herself to task and ended the conversation by asking brightly, 'Did you have a moment to go to the estate agents?'

A wide smile spread over Malcolm's face. 'I did; I've got particulars of several properties, and one is in Ebrington!'

'No!' she said in disbelief.

'The owners have inherited a considerable amount of money and a villa in the south of France. I thought we might go and look at it outside this evening, but now you're on call. . .well——'

'Oh, Malcolm, I'm so sorry, but I couldn't very well refuse in the circumstances.'

'Good heavens, of course not. I've got an order to view, but it's by appointment, so we'll try to fit in a time tomorrow evening.'

Her voice was enthusiastic. 'Ideal if it can be arranged.'

'Leave it to me,' he said airily.

Gina thought how lucky she was. Malcolm was a man who could lead, and make one feel that everything would be all right in his hands. She looked at him lovingly and saw his eyes light up as they met hers. She returned his kiss, and put her head on his shoulder as she said, 'You're so good to me.'

'I love you,' he said simply as he let her go.

They sat quietly together that evening and watched the sun set until it was a circle of flame in a sea of crimson, amber and blue. Gina told herself that here was peace and security, and that she was a singularly fortunate woman.

The telephone didn't ring once.

Paul Emerson was allowed 'home' in Erin's care, with the further support of Adrian's name. He took away with him a note which read:

Head Injury Warning
Notice

Despite a careful examination by the doctor, no significant abnormality has been found. However, all patients who have suffered a head injury should be observed over a few days for any of the following:

1. Persistent vomiting

2. Undue drowsiness or coma
3. A squint
4. Any weakness or paralysis of the limbs
5. Any deterioration in the condition

Should any of these symptoms occur, please contact your own doctor or return to the hospital.

He didn't develop any of those symptoms and it was merely a matter of the scalp laceration healing. He remained at the hotel in preference to staying at Mill Lodge, while very appreciative of Hugh's offer.

Gina learnt from Adrian that Paul Emerson was a director of a computer firm—its head office in London where he was now living—and a new branch was opening in Cheltenham, which meant his moving there, or thereabouts. He had mixed business with pleasure in coming to see Erin and Adrian, and his presence seemed further to cement that relationship.

It was five days after the accident that Erin rang Gina and asked if she would come to see her that evening. Nothing to do with medicine.

Gina agreed. Malcolm had a committee meeting and she would be on her own. Her thoughts swung to the house at Ebrington, which she and Malcolm had seen and liked, the disadvantage being that it was on the small side, leaving them in two minds about the desirability of buying it.

To Gina's amazement Adrian was at Erin's cottage when she arrived, and the thought flashed immediately to her mind that she had been invited there to be told of his and Erin's engagement. There was no sign of Paul Emerson. Perhaps he had already returned to London.

Gina had the feeling that she was waiting for the curtain to go up on a play, as Adrian poured out a dry sherry for her. Their eyes met for a fraction of a second as he placed the glass on a side-table by her chair, but his expression was unfathomable. When they were settled, Adrian and Erin on a chintz-covered sofa immediately opposite her, Gina felt she was holding her breath as Erin began, 'You must have wondered about my life, Gina.'

The words fell on a moment of tense silence.

Gina was conscious of Adrian's gaze, which was steady and unnerving, but she didn't pretend as she said frankly, 'Well, yes, I have. You seem to be a mystery.' Her pulse quickened.

'I've been a coward. And now Adrian wants you to know the truth.'

Gina's hands clenched in her lap; those few words were loaded, and could mean only one thing: that Erin and Adrian were lovers. It was, Gina knew, quite irrational, but she dreaded that relationship more than marriage, for it would strike at the very foundation of her own failed marriage and confirm the haunting fears against which she had desperately fought. All she said was a rather breathless, 'Oh!'

Erin went on quickly, 'You see, it's Paul. . .we've been lovers for five years.'

Gina gasped, '*Paul Emerson!*' In that moment thoughts rushed up at her from all sides, and none so devastating as the memory of her last conversation with Adrian on the subject of Erin. Her gaze met Adrian's and his was one of relief and resignation.

'And,' Erin added sadly, 'he's married. Adrian is the

only person who knows. He's helped me through so much, and I've trespassed on his friendship, but,' her voice faltered, 'there are times when one gets desperate. . .you see, there's no question of divorce. Paul's wife, Maud, has multiple sclerosis and is in a wheelchair. It's affected her mind, and any upset——' She made a helpless gesture.

Gina said sympathetically, 'I'm so *sorry*——'

'It's a matter of snatching hours, and without Adrian's friendship—well, it would have been impossible.' She looked at Gina with directness and honesty. 'I didn't want you to be told, but now that you've met Paul and been so helpful. . . Adrian's right; it's only fair that you should be put in the picture.'

'Thank you.' Gina looked at Adrian. 'I wish I'd known before.'

'One can never break a confidence,' he said quietly.

'Secrecy is so essential,' Erin explained. 'It wasn't a happy marriage, even before Paul and I met, and there was talk of a divorce after two years' separation; then the illness struck—badly. There's no prognosis— remissions, but she deteriorated rapidly. She has a resident nurse and Paul seems able to do more with her than anyone else. Our time together is counted in hours. But better hours with someone you love than a lifetime with someone you don't. I came here to Chipping Campden when we knew he was coming to Cheltenham. It's near enough and, above all, Adrian is here. Maud understands the name Adrian in her more normal moments, so that he can telephone Paul and keep me in touch. We don't write letters, or take any chances. So,' she finished, 'now you know, Gina, and I hope you'll understand.'

Gina's voice rang with sincerity as she said, 'I understand, and if there's ever anything I can do to help. . .'

'Thank you,' Erin murmured, and her eyes were suspiciously bright.

'Has Mr Emerson left?' Gina asked.

'Yes,' came the sad reply.

Gina looked at Adrian and recalled the incident when she had seen him with his arms around Erin. No doubt he had been comforting her when she was probably going through a bad patch. How simple the truth made it all, mocking her suspicions and highlighting her attitude generally. Equally that set off another train of thought: Adrian had been free of all emotional entanglements during this time. A flush rose in her cheeks as she thought how easy it would have been for him to ask her to remarry him after their night together. How blatantly this proved that she was no more to him than an ex-wife in whom he had no emotional interest! His relationship with Erin was, in the light of this disclosure, purely brotherly. He sat there saying little. It was impossible to tell what he was thinking.

Erin's voice had an urgency about it as she said, 'Paul must get a house in or near Cheltenham, so he'll be back, and when he's finally settled, things will be easier. I came on ahead here, as it were. He had to go to America on business and so he's been away recently.'

'If there's anything I can do in the direction of houses,' Gina said helpfully.

'Adrian's already in touch with some agents. We can sort the wheat from the chaff, and save Paul time. He needs a house that will lend itself to alterations to allow for an invalid.'

A strange sensation flowed over Gina in that moment as it struck her that, because Erin was in love with Paul, it did not cancel out the possibility that Adrian was in love with Erin. It was easy to explain their relationship by introducing the brotherly phase. And even if the friendship between Adrian and Paul was stressed, it still didn't preclude a deeper tie where Erin was concerned. If that was so, Adrian's true feelings at that moment must be very mixed. A wave of sympathy went out towards him, which struck her as ironical. Adrian must feel very isolated when faced with the deep love which Paul and Erin had for each other. It made sense to think he could bear that situation rather than disappear from her life.

Gina reflected in that moment how fortunate she was to have Malcolm's love and a future full of promise. She must not think of Adrian emotionally, nor allow her heart to quicken its beat the moment his eyes met hers. Erin was certainly a major factor in his life, even if he was not in love with her, and she must remember that. She was grateful that he had wanted her to know the truth. It seemed conciliatory and cut through the recent dissension between them. She could not help wondering how, had she known the truth about Erin and Paul, it might have influenced her actions not merely recently, but in the past. Erin had always been a shadowy, mysterious figure lurking in the background. . .and all the time she had a lover!

The question fell from her lips involuntarily and was the last she had intended asking, 'Why, Erin, didn't you want me to know about you and Paul?'

'I didn't want anyone to know. Only you and Adrian know now. If Maud were well and the whole thing could be resolved, it would be different. I just didn't want to be the woman with the married man, either condemned or pitied, or both. Adrian was different. I was thankful to be able to confide in him and I swore him to secrecy, knowing he'd never betray my trust. It wasn't anything personal between you and me, Gina; and when you were divorced and. . .well, I didn't think we should meet again. Now I'm glad you know, and that Adrian insisted on it.'

'I'm glad too,' Gina said resolutely. She felt Adrian's gaze intently upon her and there was a questioning look in his eyes which disarmed her, so that she lowered her gaze nervously and wondered why he should only now have insisted that she be told the facts. Had her words, '*Is* it the past?' been responsible? And why should love make one such a poor psychologist? Also, was she being one now, by contemplating for one moment that he was in love with Erin and ready to do anything for her, no matter how painful, rather than go out of her life?

Questions, always questions, to which she could not find an answer.

Gina was startled a few days later when Adrian asked, quite out of context, 'Have you and Malcolm settled on your house yet? He mentioned the one at Ebrington, but you were having doubts.' He looked at her with directness as he spoke, and she felt unnerved by his seriousness.

'It's rather small.'

'But bigger than a flat,' he suggested significantly.

She countered immediately, before giving herself time to think, 'Our flat was small when it came to the number of rooms, but the rooms were large.'

'Ah,' he said, 'that's true.'

'I like space. . .but Ebrington is ideal, and we're certainly unlikely to get another house for sale there.'

'Compromise,' he said.

'But not when it comes to buying something you hope to spend the rest of your days in.'

'Um-m.' It was an understanding sound, and Gina studied him intently. Since the scene with Erin a few days previously he had been pleasant and devoid of all cynicism. The battle was over and she was thankful for the harmony again, although in many ways it was harder to stifle her love for him and live up to her resolution to think of him, and treat him, just as a colleague.

'It would be very easy to let enthusiasm defeat common sense.' She added, rather too brightly, 'We want a family, and that means a family house that will seem almost too large to begin with.'

There was a sudden silence, which he broke with the warning, 'The great thing is not to rush into folly. Something you want for life must be right to begin with.'

Their eyes met.

Gina clasped her hands, which were trembling. 'One can always change houses.' She added, 'It isn't a life or death matter.'

And, although no word was said, she knew they were thinking of marriage. The past lay between them uneasily.

'The cliché that things work out,' he said, and his voice was almost grave.

'We come back to compromise,' she reminded him.

He looked doubtful. 'Neither you nor I are particularly enamoured with that word,' he said significantly.

'And neither you nor I are on holiday,' she remarked briskly. 'Talking about houses won't take care of surgery.'

'No,' he agreed. And they went their respective ways.

It was the following evening, when Malcolm and Gina had settled down in her flat with their drinks, that the front doorbell rang, and she said with a sigh as she went to answer it, 'Some emergency, no doubt.'

But Adrian stood on the threshold.

CHAPTER ELEVEN

GINA stared at Adrian as though he were an appar-
ition, her eyes full of apprehension and enquiry.

'Is Malcolm with you?'

She puckered her brows as she answered, 'Yes.'

'Can I come in?' There was a resolution about him
as he stood there with no word of apology for
interrupting.

'Of course.'

His arm brushed hers as he entered, his gaze intently
upon her.

Her pulse quickened as she said in a breath, 'Is
anything wrong?'

'Nothing that can't be put right,' he answered mys-
teriously as they reached the sitting-room.

Malcolm got to his feet and exclaimed, 'Adrian!'

Gina sat down, indicating an armchair to Adrian.
She and Malcolm shared the sofa.

The silence in the room seemed alive, and Gina
trembled. She knew that dogged look on Adrian's face,
and his manner suggested that he was in no mood to
be trifled with, whatever he had come to say. He
accepted a whisky, and when Malcolm put the glass
down on the side-table he took a sip, then said pur-
posefully, his voice strong and resonant, 'I've come for
my wife—only the law divorced us and we've been
playing at life, not only since then, but before.' He

added with passionate intensity, 'I love her and she loves me!'

Gina gave a little gasp; a shiver went over her body as she met Adrian's mesmeric, challenging gaze, and realised the full implication of his statement.

Malcolm sat there, stunned.

Adrian went on apologetically, 'I'm sorry, Malcolm, but I thought this was the most direct and responsible way of dealing with the matter and resolving the problem.'

And still Gina did not speak. Her emotions were too chaotic and churned up. Those three words 'I love her', transformed her world. She met Adrian's eyes in a look of intensity and passion which she could not withhold, nor he misunderstand.

Malcolm felt a great sadness as he said, 'I'll accept that; but aren't you taking Gina for granted?' No matter what his reactions, he had to be absolutely sure of his ground.

The question hung dangerously as Adrian said, 'Only Gina can give you an answer.'

Malcolm turned his gaze on Gina, who sat paralysed by emotion that seemed to render her incapable of speech, until she heard his words, '*Are* you still in love with Adrian?'

Gina's reply seemed to come from the depths of her being, and it was like a great burden being lifted from her shoulders as she admitted, 'Yes. . . Oh, Malcolm— I'm so sorry too.'

Adrian's eyes darkened; he didn't need to speak as he met her gaze. The problems of a lifetime seemed to have been settled by a simple statement of fact.

Malcolm got to his feet and stood looking down on

them as he said, finding truth in the wreckage and the courage to admit it, 'My head has always known, but my heart denied it. I've spent nights, recently, wondering how I could break our engagement. . .'

Gina cried 'Oh, no! You suffering too.' Her voice broke on a note of sadness.

'It's all right,' he said quietly. 'I knew for certain when we started to get a house. . .we too were playing a part—you believing that marriage to me would put Adrian out of your heart, and I trying to delude myself that I could be happy with a wife who was still in love with her ex-husband. When it came to it, I wasn't prepared to be second best. Our marriage would have been a disaster. Oh, I know I'm considered to be an easygoing sort of chap, but the pretence would have broken us both in the end.'

Gina lowered her gaze and looked at her hands, facing up to all the conflicting emotions the three of them had endured during the past months. The suspicion, jealousy, doubting that had undermined their lives.

'There are no words to say how I feel, Malcolm.' Her voice was low.

He looked at her with great gentleness. 'You loved me, but you weren't *in* love with me, and that little word encompasses a different world from just loving. I clung to the belief, too, that if you, Adrian, married Erin, things would be simple——'

Adrian stiffened, but his voice held understanding as he said, 'Erin has *never* been in my life except as a friend.'

Malcolm looked apologetic. 'One clutches at straws.'

'I was responsible for that,' Gina said quietly, and

faint colour stole into her cheeks as she met Adrian's significant gaze.

'My actions,' Adrian admitted, 'were open to misconstruction. Everything is simple with hindsight.' He looked at Malcolm with a steady, hopeful expression in his eyes. 'Is it possible to continue our friendship—the three of us?' He added earnestly, 'Or is that asking too much?'

Malcolm didn't hesitate, and his words held warmth. 'I should indeed be bereft if I lost that. This is a clean break with no misconceptions.'

Further words on the subject were not necessary.

'One other thing, Gina,' Malcolm said quickly, 'I'd like you to keep your ring—a token of friendship. I'm sure Adrian won't have any objection.'

Adrian assured him, 'By all means.'

Malcolm deliberately removed the ring and slipped it on to her right hand. 'Wear it sometimes,' he said quietly. 'I should never give it away, and I'm not arrogant enough to think I know the future.'

Adrian's voice was husky. 'May you find a happiness that seems impossible now. . .'

And although a knife was turning in Malcolm's heart he did not cancel out the likelihood, as it would have been so easy to do. He forced a half-smile as he said, 'And now I'm going to leave you. You have all my good wishes. May the future redeem the past. Thank you,' he added, looking at Adrian, 'for being so frank.'

'Brutally frank!' Adrian exclaimed. 'But, as I saw it, the only way to prevent long and painful explanations.'

Malcolm nodded and, stooping, kissed Gina's forehead, saying to himself, 'Farewell to a dream. I'll see myself out,' he added, and was gone.

They could almost hear the silence in the flat when the front door closed. Adrian moved to the sofa and took Gina in his arms.

Passion, desire, thankfulness and disbelief merged with ecstasy as he parted her lips, his kiss at first tender, then fierce and demanding as she pressed close to him with an almost frantic intensity.

He looked deeply into her eyes. 'Will you remarry me?' His voice was solemn.

'Yes—oh, yes!' she whispered as their lips met again.

They were married ten days later by special licence at the fine Chipping Campden church. It was a simple ceremony with Hugh, Anne, Jill and Erin there. Malcolm had written a short note of good wishes, adding that he hoped to see them on their return from Sherborne in Dorset, near which they were spending their honeymoon.

Anne, with understanding, had arranged a modest buffet, knowing that they wanted to get away and could not celebrate because Adrian was driving. Gina's parents were content with the fact that the newlyweds would spend a weekend of their honeymoon with them at Dunster, which was less than an hour and a half from Sherborne.

To Gina the entire day had been like a dream, and she only touched reality as Adrian's car eventually turned into the short drive of the Manor Hotel on the outskirts of Sherborne. It was a fine Elizabethan building, with mullioned windows, that lifted itself out of the surrounding undulating countryside like an ancestral home.

'Oh, Adrian—it's beautiful!' she exclaimed.

'A patient recommended it some time ago and I promised myself a visit.' He stopped the car outside the door. 'Little did I think I should be spending a second honeymoon here. . . This is even more exciting than the first,' he added as he unfastened his seatbelt and flashed Gina an adoring smile.

The hall porter hurried to help her out of the car.

They went into the fine entrance hall with its sweeping staircase and landing, from which one could look down on the scene below. It was oak-panelled, and the large windows were hung with rich red velvet. But to Gina only Adrian was real as she stood beside him while he signed the register, charming the receptionist, and then nodding to the porter who had attended to their luggage and taken the key, so that he could show them to their room—a large drawing-room-like apartment, with a four-poster bed hung in blue and pink brocade, and a view overlooking the landscaped acres, with its sweeping lawns, yew hedges, and flower-beds that were a rainbow of colour.

And at last they were alone. Gina felt that her heartbeats must be audible in her happiness as Adrian said, 'Your idea that I shouldn't make love to you until after the ceremony was diabolical!'

She gave him a little adoring and provocative smile. 'I'll never know how I've endured it either.'

'And yet,' he said, his dark eyes meeting hers, emphasising the sensuality of the moment, 'I'm glad we can savour these first hours. They're so very special.'

Gina knew that what he said was true, and she looked at him, seeing the man—powerful, commanding. Her *husband*. All the doubts and uncertainties of years vanished like a mist on a golden autumn day.

'There's so much I want to say, to ask,' she murmured, noticing the champagne in its ice-bucket which Adrian had ordered to be ready.

'We've had so much to arrange in this short while, and thank heaven we found a locum to help Hugh, otherwise we shouldn't be here.' With that Adrian reached her in a stride, his lips sinking into the yielding warmth of her mouth, their bodies pressed hard against each other.

'I want you so desperately,' he whispered, his lips moving to her neck, his hand cupping her breast.

Eyes looked into eyes, as they began to undress and finally sank down in the softness of the bed, passion mounting as his hands caressed her, making her shiver with the ecstasy of desire, before he took her in a wild rapture of surrender, as their bodies fused and the climax came in a breathless cry of emotion.

'*Darling*,' he murmured a few seconds later, as he slid down beside her and cradled her head on his shoulder, eyes meeting eyes in a moment which was full of tenderness and love. And in that moment Gina knew a happiness so deep that it filled her soul.

'When did you realise that you loved me?' she asked, slipping her left arm around his neck.

'When you wanted to tell Malcolm the truth about us,' he replied, adding, 'but I'd blinded myself until then. It would have been so easy to tell you I loved you that night we spent together, but I didn't want to delude myself after all that had happened.' He looked down at her as she raised her head from his shoulder. 'And you? When did you know?'

'The engagement party. I looked across the room at you and knew it had always been you.'

The warmth of their bodies stole sensuously between them and he held her in a vicelike grip, his lips on her forehead.

'What fools we've been!' he sighed.

'It's all been worth it,' her arm tightened around his neck, 'for this moment.' Her body pressed closer, and her voice had a little provocative note in it. 'How and why were you so certain that I loved you? Very conceited!'

'That's simple. You were so jealous of Erin! And only a woman in love could be roused to antagonism the moment I said anything she didn't agree with. Elementary, my dear Watson!'

'Conceit!' she tossed at him, smiling.

'It got us here, my darling.'

Gina repeated the endearment. 'No one can say "darling" like you.'

'I've never said it to anyone but you since we were first married,' he told her quietly.

'Neither have I. . .and so that there shall be no misunderstanding: Malcolm and I were never lovers. I deluded myself that I'd feel differently once we were married.'

He took her hand and kissed her wedding-ring—the one she had been married with the first time.

'I love you,' she said on a sigh of happiness. As she spoke she lifted herself on one elbow and looked down at his bronzed, fit body, and although she knew it as she knew her own it was suddenly and magically new.

In turn he gazed at her firm young breasts and her perfect figure. Their intimacy was so right: body and mind merging into a fulfilment that had a new dimension.

'I've learned a great deal since we were divorced.'
Adrian spoke earnestly. 'Above all, that you can't
separate two people who've been married and are still
in love.'

'I agree,' she said solemnly. 'The bond can never be
broken.'

And she went back into his arms.

— MEDICAL ♥ ROMANCE —

The books for your enjoyment this month are:

A DREAM WORTH SHARING Hazel Fisher
GIVE BACK THE YEARS Elisabeth Scott
UNCERTAIN FUTURE Angela Devine
REPEAT PRESCRIPTION Sonia Deane

♥   ♥   ♥   ♥   ♥

Treats in store!

Watch next month for the following absorbing stories:

CARIBBEAN TEMPTATION Jenny Ashe
A PRACTICAL MARRIAGE Lilian Darcy
AN UNEXPECTED AFFAIR Laura MacDonald
SURGEON'S DAUGHTER Drusilla Douglas